About the author

Constance MacKenzie always wondered, "what if?" She loved to imagine great evils roaming the earth and heroines who would come to battle. She was always confident that good trumps evil – although sometimes at a great personal cost! This is exemplified in her first novel, *Deadly Disclosure*.

Constance taught for thirty-five years in rural Saskatchewan with more than half of her career spent in Grenfell. She left teaching early in her career when her dad suffered a heart attack. She decided to farm fulltime without any experience! This almost gave her dad another heart attack! During this period, she married a farmer and had a son, Andrew. After her divorce, Constance returned to teaching and earned her Master of Education. It was during this time she first experienced the rewards of having her works published! Constance currently resides in Saskatoon, Saskatchewan to be closer to her son and his family.

www.constancemackenzie.com

DEADLY DISCLOSURE

Constance MacKenzie

DEADLY DISCLOSURE

Vanguard Press

VANGUARD PAPERBACK

© Copyright 2024
Constance MacKenzie

The right of Constance MacKenzie to be identified as author of
this work has been asserted by her in accordance with the
Copyright, Designs and Patents Act 1988.

A CIP catalogue record for this title is available from the British Library.

ISBN 978-1-83794-163-6

Vanguard Press is an imprint of
Pegasus Elliot Mackenzie Publishers Ltd.
www.pegasuspublishers.com

First Published in 2024

Vanguard Press
Sheraton House Castle Park
Cambridge England

Printed & Bound in Great Britain

Acknowledgements

Thanks to my grandson, Colin MacKenzie for his
cover design idea!

Now

Light beams, dazzlingly bright, flashing red, white, and blue, like strobe lights penetrating the darkness, searching, seeking. Accompanying these lights is the sensation of being weightless, of being gently lifted up and carried towards oblivion. Peacefulness washes over me, then nothing.

Suddenly, loud sounds, cries, shouts, and then red-hot skewers of pain slice through my unconsciousness! What? Where? Panic. My mind is screaming in pain. Why can't someone help me? Help! I try to scream, but I emit no sound.

Blackness. Peacefulness. Tranquility. Weightlessness.

***

I find myself sitting on a wooden dock, one that juts out over a body of dark, calm water. Is this a lake? I am not able to tell, as the water seems to have merged into a very dense fog. I find comfort in the warm mist that blankets me. When I become aware of my feet touching something warm and wet, I feel no anxiety, only serenity. I sigh contentedly, thinking that the lake water is like a tub of warm bathwater.

"Where am I?" I say half to myself and half to the emptiness around me. I expect no answer. I sense that here, wherever *here* is, is exactly where I am supposed to be. I am tired, so very tired. Perhaps I should just lay down on this warm dock and rest while I listen to the soft lapping of water underneath the wooden slats. I feel peaceful here. I feel so safe, so contented. Contentedness is an unusual feeling for me; my whole life I always questioned everything and everyone – but not now. Here I am comforted. I surprise myself with my inability to think of even one question worth asking. Slowly, I succumb to the temptation of lying down – the dock feels warm and welcoming underneath me.

***

Blinding, searing hot pain slashes through me!

"We got her back!" an excited voice exclaims. I feel a hand squeezing my shoulder. "Don't leave us, Cathy; fight, come back to us!"

Darkness.

Then

My day started the same as most of my warm spring days in southern Alberta. It found me lying outside on our patchy green lawn, which, if its colors were black and white instead of green and brown, would look more like a rug made from the hide of a Holstein dairy cow. I was reading a romance novel, my favorite genre for the last couple of years. I was a teenager, and I was no longer interested in children's novels. I enjoyed spending my free time reading and daydreaming about these quixotic fictional characters who overcame obstacles no matter how daunting; and always – yes, always – finding true love.

My family and I lived in a very small, very ugly, faded blue one-and-a- half-story house. My brothers shared the large upstairs bedroom, while I had a very small bedroom, more like a large closet, across the hall from them. Our house was situated in a very small town in southern Alberta. The town had a catchy name, Purple Springs. I always thought it was some pioneer's idea of a bad joke. It hardly ever rained here, which was okay by me, but the local water supply was also not very good. The town's water was pumped up from a very deep well that was saturated with harsh minerals – safe for human consumption, we were told. Often, the water filling the bathtub smelled like stagnant slough water! If that wasn't bad enough, summer often resulted in water rationing. To have a spring that supplied purple water, perhaps purple Kool-Aid would have been as likely as having plenty of questionable water throughout the summer!

My mom and dad's names are Elizabeth and Frank Parker. My older brother's name is Lawrence, and my younger brother's name is Jay.

Lawrence is fifteen, and he is already studying for his learner's license, a fact that he never ceases to boast about. Jay is eleven years old and studying how to be more obnoxious than Lawrence. I am a very mature thirteen-year-old young lady. Our closeness in age should make us friends, but it has not.

I detest my brothers. Too strong? Let me tell you why, and maybe you, too, would share my low opinion of my siblings. They constantly tease, they constantly get out of work, and they constantly receive preferential treatment from my parents.

Mom and Dad are very close. They do everything together. Often, they even think the same thought at the very same time! Yet, as in any group of people, whether it's two or fifty, there is a hierarchy of power with someone at the top, someone who has the final say. My family's veto power goes directly to Mom. She uses it periodically, but I notice I am the recipient of her wisdom more often than my brothers. Enough said about my family's dynamics!

On this momentous day, I heard Dad's car's rough-sounding engine grow louder and louder as it traveled down our street towards home. He's driving faster than usual, my analytical brain pointed out without emotion or concern. Dad was arriving home from working at the sugar beet factory much quicker than usual. Dad often said that his job was so simple that a monkey would be able to do it! Tires crunched on what was left of our scantily graveled driveway. Dad's usual slow, heavy footsteps were replaced by quicker, eager footsteps. Something was up! I could feel it in the air! I put down my novel and ran around to the front of the house, where I greeted my dad with, "Hi, Dad! What's up?"

"Oh, just something that might change your whole life!" he said, laughing as he hugged me. Dad paused and added in a more serious tone, "You stay out here; I want to talk to Ma alone!" I was excited for no real reason. It felt like it was Christmas morning, yet that was months away!

"Okay," I said, feeling left out. My face reflected my jilted feelings.

"I won't be long," said Dad with a wink of his eye, "then we'll call you inside to hear the news. You're going to love it!" Dad's tone reflected the same excitement I was feeling a moment before.

I watched my dad enter the house with a letter clutched in his right hand. I was no longer interested in my romance novel; I just had to find out what was happening. I quickly walked over to the front room window. I crouched under it, where I hoped to hear some of their conversation. I strained my ears to hear. Try as hard as I could, I failed to discern any intelligible sound from the house.

"Cathy! Cathy, come here!" my mom's voice sounded from the back door of our house. I was off like a shot, running for the door. I didn't stop until I reached the living room, where my parents were sitting on the well-used flower print couch. "Come here, Cathy. Sit down. We are just waiting for your brothers to get here."

I settled myself on my favorite soft brown floor cushion. What news could possibly change my life? *Probably Mom is going to have another baby*, whispered a tiny, irritated voice in my head. Yuck! It would probably be another boy! I felt miserable. My logical voice pointed out: wouldn't they be worried if there was to be another baby? I often heard about how tight our money was whenever I wanted something. It had to be something else!

My internal debate was abruptly interrupted by my brothers' arrival. They ran into the living room and asked in unison, "What's up?"

Mom motioned for them to sit down on the rug beside me.

Dad cleared his throat and started. "You know that Gramps and Grams are getting older…"

My heart lurched; no, don't tell me something has happened! My heart started to break.

Dad's excited voice interrupted my fears with the words, "Moving to British Columbia! They want me to take over the farm… er, to rent it from them. To help us out, they will give us the yard, house, buildings, and machinery! Your mom and I have decided to do this, but only if you guys are on board, too. Well?" Mom and Dad looked at each of us, waiting for our response.

The silence in the room was miraculous! I never thought I would witness the day my brothers were struck speechless! Dad and Mom looked at each other. Mom added, "You know, kids, Dad's farm has been in the family for four generations! It is like preserving a part of your family history!"

"Why haven't we ever been to Gramps' farm?" asked Lawrence, first to get his voice back.

"Well, it is kind of a long story," started Dad. "When I was a little older than you, Lawrence, I got into, er, some trouble. I decided to move away with your Mom."

"We have never returned," continued Mom, blushing. Dad and Mom looked at each other, smiled and held hands. "That is why Gramps and Grams always came here to visit. We just didn't see the sense in returning to the farm…"

"Until now," finished Dad.

"Where is this farm?" asked Jay.

"It is three miles outside of a small hamlet," stated Mom.

"Smaller than Purple Springs?" I queried.

"Yes, much smaller," said Mom. "Its name is Keysound."

"Never heard of it," my brothers mumbled together.

Laughing, Dad said, "Nor has most of the world!"

I was excited about the idea of farming. The pioneer spirit was beginning to stir inside of me, where only moments ago tears were starting to well up in my eyes.

Mom continued, "If Dad isn't interested, then the family farm is to be sold."

"We're moving to Saskatchewan! We are going to be farmers!" I cheered. My brothers excitedly agreed, the second miracle inside of an hour!

Mom and Dad stood up and motioned my brothers and me to come to them for one of our family hugs. Our lives here were over, our new lives were beginning. There was no turning back now. We were moving east to Saskatchewan, our sister province.

"When?" asked Jay.

"We move at the end of the school year," said Mom and Dad together. "Spring seeding will be starting soon," continued Dad, "so I will be leaving on the weekend to get things in order. I'll be back and forth till the crop is planted."

**

Our small, mini convoy of two trucks that Gramps gave us proceeded down country gravel roads, turning right, then left. Dad led the way, driving the four-ton truck with Lawrence seat-belted beside him. Mom followed behind, driving the smaller one-ton truck with Jay and me – I sat beside the door after pulling rank – I was older, after all! Mom geared down, slowing our progress as we neared our new yard which had expanded from a town lot of a hundred feet by ninety feet to a yard of five acres!

The first thing I saw from the truck's window was the distant trees – tall, bushy and dark green, green so dark that it appeared more black than green. It looked like a large planter overgrown with foliage had been set down at the edge of a planted field. This wall of dense greenery appeared to have pierced the low-lying, heavy-looking nimbostratus rain clouds. Peering out between the clouds were patches of very dark blue sky. These heavy-looking clouds appeared ready to dump gallons of water on us without a moment's notice. The wind, as if on cue, started to stir these huge branches growing out from massive tree trunks. It looked more like green monsters waving their arms, welcoming us – or were they warning us to turn around and get away as fast as possible? I was in awe and somewhat worried about my new life. My pioneer excitement once more bubbled up through my mind, dislodging these feelings of apprehension.

Smoothly, the trucks geared down, their speeds slowed. One after the other we slowly turned left onto the driveway. To me, the driveway looked more like a tongue sticking out from this green monster's mouth.

Unexpectedly, I remembered my best friend, Mary. She would always stick her tongue out when she was happy. A fleeting sense of sadness over the loss of my best friend touched my heart, and once more my excitement was momentarily dampened.

Gradually, the trucks drove deeper into the forested yard. Tires crunched on the thickly graveled driveway. Abruptly, the trees yielded to spacious lawns and high, bushy hedges that needed trimming. The trucks halted beside a large ranch-style house. The white and brown trim four-bedroom bungalow looked neat and smart under the ever-diminishing afternoon sun.

As if planned, we all got out of our vehicles together, stretched, and looked about. "We're home!" whooped Lawrence and Jay, as they started running around the yard, trying to tag each other.

"Oh, Frank!" exclaimed Mom, "I can hardly believe that this is all ours!"

Mom and Dad hugged each other as they stood admiring our new home. I decided not to waste any more time outside.

I marched proudly up to the white wooden door, opened it, and entered my new home.

Its interior was warm, comfortable, and inviting. I slowly moved from the small entranceway into a large ranch-style kitchen. Huge cupboards with their doors ajar stood patiently waiting to be filled once more with plates, glasses, mugs, pots, and pans. 'Welcome to your new home,' they silently whispered to me. 'Look around. Make yourself at home.'

"Thanks, I will," I whispered back.

"Who are you talking to?" asked Dad, who had just entered with an extra-large, heavy-looking box.

"Oh, just the house," I grinned. My immediate objective was clear in my mind, so, without another word, I set off to find and claim my bedroom before my brothers took the best bedrooms for themselves.

"Elizabeth," Dad addressed my mom, "do you think your daughter is feeling all right?"

"Oh, Frank," laughed Mom, "she has always had an overactive imagination!"

I smiled.

Now

"She's starting to come back to us," an excited voice announces.

"No!" I shout, as my parents start to fade. Tears stream out of my eyes. "Please come back," I moan desolately.

"What did she say?"

"She must be in pain. It's time for another shot of fentanyl." A gentle hand strokes my face.

Blackness.

Then

I zeroed in, like a guided missile, on a light green room at the entrance to our house's sole hallway. The light green walls were accented with a warm brown wood trim. The floor was covered with linoleum; the original color had faded to an off-white. I entered this room to look out its sole large window. Delighted, I discovered that it looked out over a huge flower garden. I saw that the multitude of flowers were in different stages of blooming. I saw blooms fully opened, displaying petals of various sizes and shapes and colors. I noticed that over half of the flower garden had green round, ball-like flower buds that were slow to open, preferring to keep hidden their colorful petals tightly wrapped within. "Perfect!" I exclaimed.

"Why, Cathy," chuckled Dad, who had appeared in the bedroom's doorway holding a large heavy-looking box in his hands, "since you like it, this room will be yours. Lawrence will have the room at the end of the hallway. Jay will get the room across from Lawrence! Our bedroom is across from you. The main bathroom is between Lawrence's and your bedrooms. Your mother and I have our own ensuite bathroom, so you kids have the main bathroom to yourselves! Now make yourself useful and help unload the trucks before it rains!" Dad left and went into my parents' bedroom, where he deposited the box he was carrying.

I smiled and hurried back outside to where the sky, appearing as a living mischievous creature, had pulled together the dark rain clouds, like blackout drapes over a window. The beautiful dark blue sky of moments ago was completely gone! *Wow!* I marveled to myself, *Saskatchewan's white license plates' logo, 'The Land of Living Skies', printed in green letters, was evidently very accurate!*

Now

Bone-crushing pressure. Can't breathe! Futile attempt to get out from under the repeatedly rhythmic pressure crushing my chest. Need to breathe. Breathe! Panic is notched up to its maximum heart-stopping setting.

"We've got a heartbeat, it's faint and thready," comes an indistinct voice from very far away.

"Check. Get the oxygen going," quickly adds another impersonal voice. I feel a cold piece of smooth material touch my face.

"Oxygen saturation is ninety-eight percent."

A cool wisp of air tickles my nose. Instinctively, I suck it in. Greedily, I take another breath, then another. My mind calms. My panic quickly fades.

"Thank you," I murmur.

"That's a better mix," states a voice that seems to be coming from very far away.

"Ready for transport."

"Check," comes another voice, barely audible. Then blackness. Peacefulness. Weightlessness.

Then

I woke to the sound of rain gently tapping against my bedroom window. I snuggled deeper into my blankets. I listened. No street noises. No sound of the train's horn blaring as it roared through town. This silence, this living silence seemed to wrap its arms around me, nuzzling me back to sleep in my new home, in my new bedroom, in my old familiar bed.

***

I was a typical teenage girl. This unquestionably meant that I was interested in boys. However, the only boys here were my brothers or the handsome characters in my romance novels, and clearly my brothers did not count! My novels were packed into a box that had yet to be found and unpacked! I wanted to investigate each unopened box before emptying another box!

"I think your books are likely to be in one of these," Mom said with a smile as she assigned me to the duty of unpacking boxes stacked in the kitchen.

After what seemed like hours of work opening and emptying boxes, then flattening them for recycling, I failed to find the box containing my novels! I had stacked dishes, pots and pans, cutlery, and various baking dishes on our red Formica-topped kitchen table. Mom kept leveling the stacks of tableware and bakeware as cupboards and drawers were filled. I was becoming increasingly worried about the safety of my books. Did they make it to Saskatchewan? Were they forgotten in Purple Springs, maybe left sitting in my old bedroom?

Once there were no boxes left to be opened, I helped Mom store the remaining plates, bowls, and cutlery into our canary yellow cupboards, the only bright spot on this dreary rainy day. The house seemed to buzz with the sounds of ripping packing tape, the crunching of boxes for recycling, and Dad's heavy footsteps delivering packed boxes to various rooms in our new house.

A loud knock sounded on the outside wooden door, with an accompanying shout, "Frank! Frank Parker, you ol' son of a bitch! Welcome back to Keysound, Saskatchewan!" It instantly froze all our movements throughout the house.

Without waiting for Mom or Dad to open the door, a short, stout man, slightly swaying from the drink he had consumed, lumbered into the kitchen. In his left hand was a partially full mickey of Jack Daniels. Standing beside him was a boy – yes, a boy about my age! My interest piqued and my desire to find my romance novels ebbed, at least for now! This was the first boy I had seen since our move; maybe he was the only boy for miles!

He was taller than me by perhaps an inch or two. He had a square jaw (cute, I thought, but then mentally corrected myself, as boys wanted to be handsome or rugged or something like that. After all, that was how they were described in my romance novels!). His head was covered with light tousled brown hair that appeared to nip at the bottoms of his ears. He stood tall and proud beside and slightly behind his uncouth father. The boy's self-confidence emitted a strong aura around his youthful body.

Dad quickly entered the kitchen to see who was yelling his name. "Good morning!" Dad said, confusion evident on his face. "I am sorry, but I seem to have forgotten who you are!"

Chuckling, the overweight, slightly inebriated man said, "My name is Floyd. I was too busy when you were down seeding with your old man to drop in and say hi." Dad began to look uneasy when he heard his name.

"Floyd Moonie; you know, we went to school together. You saved my bacon when three mean boys were going to give me a whipping when I was in grade three!"

"Oh, yeah, little Floyd!" Dad exclaimed, his face reflecting the recollection of the event. "My God, you have changed!"

Chuckling, Floyd pointed to the boy at his side. "And this here is my boy, Horace. We live a mile west of here. We are your closest neighbors!"

Barely pausing for a breath, he pivoted to point a finger at Mom, who stood frozen with cups in her hands. "This pretty woman can't be Lizzy?"

"Yes, this is my wife Liz, my sons Lawrence and Jay, and my daughter Cathy," Dad made the introductions. My face turned red as I looked at Horace, who was grinning back at me. The grin was very magnetic, drawing me into his aura like magnetic north pulls the compass needle. I suddenly felt warm all over while my face burned. My brothers missed their opportunity to tease me, as they were too busy talking loudly and excitedly to Horace. "Kids!" Dad said. "The rain has pretty much let up, so take the noise outside! We are trying to talk in here!"

I looked at Mom, who gave me a look that said to go outside with my brothers as she would be all right making the coffee.

Relieved, I quickly caught up with them as they headed north from our house to our gigantic red barn with green shingles. It had been built in 1901 and it had been home to cattle, workhorses, and pigs. Atop of the gable end roof stood two cupolas, miniature houses painted red with white trim. Affixed to the roof of one cupola was a weathervane with a black stallion marking the wind's direction. Periodically, it moved in the light breeze, indicating the wind was coming from the north to northeast. Today, the old barn was home to Dad's newly acquired farm machinery and vehicles, the farm animals replaced and forgotten. My grandparents had installed a huge door in the east wall which opened on heavy-duty rollers.

When it was fully opened, Dad was able to drive our red tractor – a Versatile – and our New Holland combine into the barn. Each parked machine waited in the barn, like the Clydesdales of long ago, until it was once more time to go to work.

"I always loved this barn!" said Horace wistfully as he pulled open the original west-sliding door. The cool damp air from the barn's interior rushed out to meet the rain-fresh air. My brothers made a comment about the mustiness of the barn, but neither Horace nor I paid them any attention. It was as if we were enclosed in a clear bubble. We could hear the others, but we only wanted to communicate with each other. His magnetism was overpowering. I was beginning to feel like the women described in my romance novels! My heart murmured softly, "Is this love?" My wedding, our love-making, and our future kids invaded my senses while I stood with Horace in the barn's entrance.

Trying to think of something intelligent to say, I asked, "Did you come over here when Gramps and Grams lived here?"

"Oh, yes – especially when it got bad at home. I would spend days here – once as much as a week!" This broke the warm bubble around Horace and me. I felt a deep sadness for him as I thought of the love and warmth of my family, even my brothers.

"Didn't your parents mind?" asked Lawrence.

"Nah, I don't think they even missed me!" Horace replied brusquely.

We silently moved further into the old red barn, not minding the smell of wet wood and damp dirt on the cold cement floor. "Come, I'll show you a great place to slide down a chute from the loft down to the ground floor!" said Horace.

Excitedly, we ran after Horace, who was heading toward the far end of the barn. He reached a ladder that leaned against what remained of the loft's floor about seven feet above our heads. Half of the loft had been cut away by Gramps to make room to store the farm machinery. Twenty feet above our heads, the beams of the barn's roof were visible. "We have to climb this," said Horace, pointing to the rickety ladder.

"Is it safe?" asked Jay, worry evident in his voice.

Horace confidently stepped up on the ladder and began to climb, pausing once to look down at us to utter a warning, "Step over the fourth step, it's broken!"

Eagerly, we climbed the old ladder up to the amputated, mutilated old loft. The vaulted ceiling yawned thirteen feet above our heads, dwarfing us. I felt that I understood, at that moment, what a fly would feel like flying about in my bedroom. "Wow!" I exclaimed, "It is so big!" My words were drawn out in my wonder.

"Wow! It is so big!" mimicked Jay, as Lawrence laughed.

"Yes, it is impressive," added Horace, "especially when you think of men climbing up there during the barn raising! It took guts!"

My brothers quit teasing me as they looked uneasily at each other.

Eager to change the subject, Lawrence asked, "Where is this chute?"

"Over there," said Horace, pointing to the far corner. "It is behind that old trunk."

We spent the rest of the misty morning climbing the ladder, sliding down the chute and playing tag. Exhausted, we laid down on the loft floor to listen to the rain as its tempo picked up. With the rain splattering against the roof, we spoke of school, teachers, and friends. As the conversation ebbed, we were content to listen to Mother Nature humming us a lullaby. The silence was soothing, until Lawrence asked, "Horace, where do you go to school?"

"I go to Simokon." Chuckling, Horace added, "When I go!"

Later that night, I asked Dad if we could go to Simokon instead of KPS. "Why would you want to go to Simokon?" Dad wanted to know.

"She wants to be with Horace!" teased Lawrence.

"No, stupid," I shot back, "I want to go to Simokon because we know one person there and zero people in KPS!"

"Kids, quit that bickering!" shouted Mom from the kitchen. "Cathy, come out here and dry the dishes!"

"Dad, it's Jay's turn to dry dishes!" I protested.

"Cathy, do as your Mom tells you," Dad sternly countered. Dad would have made a great politician; he always sided with Mom without ever coming right out and telling me what to do!

"Great!" I yelled angrily. "You're always favoring Lawrence and Jay!" I shot Dad the angriest look I could muster and stomped loudly into the kitchen. I heard the boys snickering. Dad stopped them short when he told them to go to bed. Well, at least they didn't get to watch TV, I thought, somewhat pacified.

"But, Dad," they whined together, "what about TV?"

"Sorry, boys, no TV tonight," said Dad sternly.

***

We were having Mom's specialty – cabbage rolls. Her cabbage rolls were so tasty that people have been known to make themselves sick from overeating! Once you started eating, it was very hard to stop! It was while we ate that my parents' conversation inescapably returned to our neighbors. The Moonies seemed to have become a point of contention between my parents, something that was unheard of before our initial meeting with Floyd. "Frank, it seems that Floyd has never grown up. I think that he has gotten worse as an adult!" said Mom, after she had swallowed a forkful of her delicious hot cabbage roll.

"Floyd is Floyd," said my Dad, finishing off his second helping of cabbage rolls. "Liz, you should know that! He hasn't changed since he was in school; guess he never will." Dad wiped his mouth and pushed back from the table. I was surprised that Dad was finished, as he always had a third helping. This unexpected reaction dampened my appetite, and I began to play with the last cabbage roll on my plate.

"That is an understatement," replied Mom as she finished her first helping of cabbage rolls. "He was obnoxious in school, but he is worse now. He is rude and he drinks like a fish!" Mom said in a voice that showed she had a point to make. I noticed my brothers had also momentarily paused their eating. Unlikely as it was, we were united in our looking forward to going to the same school as Horace. I smiled, thinking that for once my brothers were going to help me get what I wanted.

I was sure the point Mom was going to make would mean I would not have any further contact with Horace. I felt miserable. Was this how Juliet felt when her family forbade her from being with Romeo? My parents, oblivious to my inner turmoil, continued to talk. Dad paused the conversation when he passed the large bowl of cabbage rolls to Lawrence. My nerves were strung so tight that I wanted to yell out, "Stop all the eating!" When the bowl of cabbage rolls was passed to me, I politely said, "No, thanks," and proceeded to pass the bowl to Mom. I had manners! I could control myself, if barely. I sat and finished off my cooled cabbage roll. My brothers had slowly resumed eating. Their knives made the only sound in the kitchen as the knife blades clicked on the plates as each perfectly formed cylindrical roll was cut into mouth-size pieces.

As my family once more began to slow down in their attack of their food, Mom picked up where she left off, not missing a beat. "I met Floyd's wife in the Co-op today. She is so tiny, just the opposite of Floyd! Do you know Sheena?"

Dad leaned back in his chair and slowly shook his head. "No, I don't really. I know she isn't from the area."

"She seems very nice, so unlike Floyd," Mom said, and Dad shot her a quizzical look.

"You know, she wasn't drunk, she wasn't offering me whiskey, she seemed coherent, and she seemed normal!"

"Floyd likes his liquor, but I have seen him sober," added my Dad in defense of Floyd.

"But, Dad," interjected Lawrence, "he offered you a beer from the back of his pickup truck today when he came by while we were changing the cultivator shovels down at the barn!"

"Yeah, and he offered us a drink, too!" Jay added excitedly.

Mom looked shocked. "Frank, you didn't let the boys drink, did you?" she asked worriedly.

"Ah gee, Mom!" whined my brothers, as Dad shook his head no. "Horace gets to drink with his dad," Lawrence continued in his best complaining voice that I have ever heard.

"That settles it! I think we better stay away from Floyd and his family," cautioned my mom. "I also think that if his kids go to the school in Simokon, our kids should go to KPS"

"Oh great, just because his dad drinks, we can't go to the one school in which we know one person!" I argued. Dad shot me a glance that told me that he knew exactly what I was meaning. My face turned red. My brothers failed to notice my look of embarrassment as they were too busy talking about meeting Horace's eighteen-year-old sister, Melissa.

***

Summer always seemed to pass by quickly, too fast for me! Each day was spent weeding the garden that the neighbors were so kind to plant for us when the news of the prodigal son's return had reached this small community. I guessed that it sounded romantic that the banished son and his wife were returning to their place of birth. It must have appealed to their whimsical natures, as the garden was of gargantuan proportions! The vegetable garden stretched forever – reminding me of the poem, *In Flanders Fields*. Is this what the rows of crosses would look like, endless? Weeds, weeds, weeds, thousands of weeds! When you looked up, you were no closer to the end of the row than you were thirty minutes earlier!

Please save me! I silently prayed.

"Kids, supper!" shouted Mom.

Thank you, Lord, for listening to me! I silently prayed. *Now, if it is not too much, please allow us to attend school in Simokon!* I offered up a promise because nothing was free, even from God! I promised not to fight with my brothers for a whole month! Deep down, I felt that I might be able to make two weeks, but it is the thought that counts, right? Dinner was going to prove that this prayer would be answered in a way that my whole life was going to be changed forever.

Supper was ready to eat; the smells were heavenly. After working in the garden for hours in the hot afternoon sun, the smell of hot food was intoxicating. I was in a good mood. My brothers were not teasing me; they were behaving like responsible humans! Maybe they had been abducted. That thought made me smile. My life was good; nothing bad could ever happen when everything seemed so right, right? The Kraft dinner, vegetables and smoked sausages were dished out. Freshly baked buns were still warm in the basket sitting in the center of the table.

"Liz," Dad had started to say. My parents had always called each other by their real names. Mom had said that this was the way she was able to keep her identity. Of course, we had called them Mom and Dad. I had asked about calling them by their real names, reciting Mom's reason back to her, but Mom just laughed and said that Mom and Dad are their real names to their children.

"I am glad we came," Mom finished for Dad.

"I am happier working for myself than working in the sugar beet factory," Dad continued with a strong sense of pride resounding in his voice. He never had this sense of fulfillment when we lived in Purple Springs. Dad sipped his coffee from his mug before he continued. "We have been invited to the community dance tonight." Dad paused and took another sip of coffee, then quickly added, "The Moonies have invited us."

"The Moonies!" Mom said tersely, putting her cup down onto the table with a thud. Some of her coffee sloshed over the edge of the mug.

"Now, Liz, they're not so bad," said Dad. "They're different, that's all. They seem nice in their own way!" Dad hurried on, "I always felt sorry for Floyd in school; he was always picked on, don't you remember? I guess I still feel kind of sorry for him." Mom stared at Dad with a look that said Floyd got what he deserved. "We will go with them, but we'll take our own vehicle so we can leave when we want to. This is a good way to get reacquainted with the neighbors. We can also meet the parents of the children our kids will be going to school with. Perhaps we can finally decide once and for all which school the kids will attend. School starts in a couple of weeks," reasoned Dad.

That was that. Dad had chalked up one of his infrequent wins with Mom! I was proud of him! The school decision was still up for review. My parents would go to the community dance with the Moonies. Tomorrow, I would be going to Simokon. I would date Horace; marry him when I leave school. We would go to university, graduate, land jobs, have kids and live happily ever after!

***

Hours later, my parents' loud, arguing voices rudely interrupted my peaceful sleep. "I have never been so embarrassed in my whole life!" hissed Mom. "What was I supposed to say when Floyd told me that Sheena had smothered her newborn son in a dresser drawer?"

"Well, I don't think telling him that his wife must have been mentally unbalanced was a good idea!" shot back Dad, his voice a harsh whisper. "Didn't you see Sheena standing there, hearing this little conversation?"

"No, I didn't!" Mom yelled in a voice that continued to be low in volume but high in emotion. "She didn't have to curse me like that; it was so vulgar, so degrading! And you, you never helped me, you just stood there looking – what? Which side were you on? It surely wasn't on my side!" Mom broke down, sobbing.

"Now, honey," Dad said soothingly, his voice lowered, "I am sorry. I just didn't expect this. My God, to kill your baby! I just didn't know what to do! What to say!" I knew Dad was holding Mom; even without seeing them. I could see them in my mind, sitting on our well-worn couch in the living room, taking comfort from each other.

"I just wish we had left right then and there," sobbed Mom.

"Me, too," assured Dad. "If only I could go back in time. I just can't believe what we have gone through. We are lucky to be alive. I have never been so fearful of staying alive in my whole life!" said Dad in an increasingly hushed voice.

Wow! My always present inquisitiveness had shot into overdrive. *Go back to sleep, don't listen to your parents, you know that you're snooping on their private conversation,* my logical brain advised. Yeah, right! I was even more determined to listen carefully. What could have scared my parents so much? I had never known my parents to be fearful of anything! I was unaware that this was the impetus that would start me down a path to a future – a future that would bring passion, love, heartbreak and near death into my life!

"I should never have let you go with Sheena," said Dad.

"She was drunk. Sheena couldn't drive home, and you were right, she was dangerous – both to herself and to Floyd," rationalized Mom.

"I just didn't know how dangerous!" bristled Dad, anger evident in his voice.

"You drove Floyd home. What happened when you got Floyd home?" asked Mom.

"It was just like a horror movie! Floyd went inside, yelling at Horace and his younger sister, Alison. He cursed them for being asleep and for being lazy! He ordered them to make breakfast for us. Can you imagine that? As if I could eat! He then demanded that Horace tell him where his older sister Melissa was. I thought Floyd was going to hit him when he said she was out on a date. I felt sick with disgust when I saw Floyd's look of jealousy on his face! I just wanted to go home, but you hadn't arrived with Sheena, so I had to wait. I didn't want you to be stranded in this repulsive situation without a way home!"

They were silent for a long time. I was beginning to think that this was all I was going to hear, when I heard Dad continue speaking softly. "Bacon and eggs will never look good to me again! Alison and Horace put together the breakfast. While they worked in silence, Floyd kept at them. I don't know if he wanted to get into a fight with them, or if he just wasn't thinking, but either way, Horace finally blew up. He yelled at his father that he was a coward, that he was a drunk, and that he was a sex deviant having sex with Melissa as well as with anything else that walked about!"

"Oh, Frank, that is terrible! I knew there was something vile about that man!" said Mom vehemently.

"That was when Floyd hit Horace so hard that I thought he had killed the boy. The lad didn't move. When I started to get up to check on the boy, Floyd warned me away! I asked him whether he cared if he killed his son. He shot back at me that since Sheena killed his first son, then why shouldn't he be able to kill the second one? I couldn't believe it! I saw the glint of insanity in his eyes and realized that he was dead serious. I backed away from Floyd. I was afraid!" Dad said softly. "I still am."

"You did the only thing you could do under the circumstances," Mom said lovingly.

I knew they'd be sitting close together, sharing each other's strength and love as they tried to make sense of what they had survived.

The house, the silence, the darkness, the lateness of the hour, all surrounded me as we waited for the rest of the story, the rest that we collectively knew was going to be worse than what had just been shared. I wished moments later that I had stayed asleep like my brothers and never heard this tale. I wished that I had never heard these hushed cold words of appalling truth.

I started to grow sleepy, when Mom's words jerked me awake.

"Sheena was very drunk and so angry, so very angry! I think she was almost insane in her hatred of Floyd. I didn't know what to say to her to soothe her emotions. I suggested that I should drive, but Sheena objected, saying that driving always helps her to calm her nerves, to relax after fighting with Floyd. I had no choice, so I walked around the front of their truck to the passenger side. I got in, while Sheena climbed in behind the steering wheel."

"I know, Liz," said Dad. "That is why I wanted you to go with her and I go with Floyd. I really did think that by doing this we would help diffuse the time bomb that I knew was ready to explode."

"Your idea was honorable, but terribly off the mark!" Mom said with a quiver in her voice.

Once more silence. The minutes ticked by. I felt isolated as I listened in on my parents' private talk. I knew how it would be like to spy on another – dirty and cheap, yet impossible to quit, like being pulled down in a quicksand of curiosity – the need to know, to understand the circumstances. Was this an insight to my future self? As I lay in my bed, barely breathing, I heard my parents move about in the living room. Dad came down the hallway toward my bedroom. "I'll check the kids, Liz," Dad told Mom as he paused outside of my bedroom door. Dad stood silently, like a cat beside a mouse hole, waiting for the mouse to stick out its head. I tried to breathe slowly and deeply, with my back towards the door. I dared not twitch when Dad opened my door. I was silhouetted in the hall's light that dimly illuminated my bedroom.

"Cathy, are you sleeping?" Dad asked softly.

I thought about this question my parents always ask. Did they ever really expect me to say, "No, Dad, I'm just snooping on your private conversation like some Peeping Tom!" I didn't say this. I just kept on breathing, as I would have been doing if I really was asleep.

Obviously, this worked, as Dad said softly, "Goodnight, lass." Softly he closed my door once more, plunging my room into total darkness.

"The kids are asleep," Dad said to Mom when he returned to the living room. I heard the couch groan under his weight as he sat down beside Mom.

"We must keep our voices down," cautioned Mom. "I don't want the kids to know this. I don't want to know this, but I guess that isn't an option anymore."

"Honey, I'm so very, very sorry for putting you in that situation," Dad softly consoled Mom. "You didn't know what Sheena was going to do. I didn't know. In fact, I don't think Sheena knew what she was going to do before your arrival at their farm."

"As I said, she was angry." Mom cleared her throat. "I thought she would calm down; in fact, she seemed to calm down as she drove. Anyway, as Sheena drove, we talked kids, farming, you know, just, well, general stuff. She talked; I listened. I was asking her about various yard lights that appeared as we drove through the dark countryside. She identified each – finally showing me theirs and then ours. I remembered thinking, as we crossed their Texas cattle gate, that I was able to calm Sheena. I felt empowered! I had saved Sheena from herself. I guess I was too relaxed and I failed to notice the change in her mood when Floyd appeared in the doorway."

"We heard the approach of the truck – you'd have a hard time missing that engine, it sputters and coughs whenever you slow down!" Dad added with a chuckle. "I didn't think anything about it when Floyd went outside – I thought that, like me, he was going outside to greet his wife, maybe apologize, you know."

Dad's words became so quiet that they were indiscernible to me. I had to chance getting out of my bed. I had a spring that always squeaked if I sat up, so I gently rolled out of bed. I tiptoed quietly toward my bedroom door and cautiously opened it a crack.

"Sheena started screaming out a litany of Floyd's sins, seasoned with the foulest language I have ever heard! She stomped down on the accelerator. The truck leapt to life. It pounced at Floyd like a charging lion. It landed where Floyd had stood seconds before! I thought he was crushed under the wheels. I remember dispassionately thinking that it was odd, I would have thought the truck would tilt, lean to one side after running over a man as big as Floyd. Before I could finish thinking about the consequences of running over Floyd, Sheena rammed the truck's gearshift into reverse and punched down on the gas pedal. My head snapped back, hitting the back window. I saw stars! I had never believed a person really did see stars! Now I know it is true!

"Once back several feet from the front door, Sheena violently braked, then threw the truck into drive and once more the truck surged forward. I hung onto the door with the death grip of a drowning man. Miraculously, the truck missed Floyd again! I can't remember how many times we were backing up and charging. Finally, I was relieved when Sheena aimed at their house! Can you imagine that, Frank? I was happy to be charging straight at their house! How crazy is that?"

Mom went silent. Dad's hushed words broke the silence. "When I heard the engine revving, the tires squealing, and the cursing, I hurried towards the open door. Floyd blew past me like a hurricane and those bright, paralyzing headlights pinned me. I felt like a spotlighted deer. I believed that my life was about to end! I was frozen in place, my muscles were paralyzed, but my brain was screaming, *Move, you idiot!* The blinding light grew so very fast! The tires started to howl like a beast caught in a trap. That is when I realized that their front steps had crumbled with the weight of the truck's front axle. The truck's front end was trapped only inches from flattening me! Thank God Floyd believed in leaving most work for tomorrow. I never knew procrastination would save my life!"

Dumbstruck by my parents' harrowing experience, I silently closed my bedroom door and returned to my bed. I rolled back onto my bed and pulled my covers up to my chin. As I drifted off to sleep, I heard the clicking of light switches throughout the house. Once again, darkness wrapped its calming arms around me and my family.

Now

Voices gently flutter down through the darkness to me like falling leaves on an autumn day. I return once more to sit on the wooden dock. As I listen to the lapping of the water underneath the wooden planks, I feel peaceful.

"Cathy."

I jerk at the unexpected sound. "Dad?" I softly call out. "Is that you?"

"Hey, little one," the soft voice comes back. I feel the love in his words, and I start to cry.

"But how? You're dead!"

"I have come to help you," my dad tells me tenderly.

"Dad, I miss you so much!" I sob.

"I miss you, too," Dad says softly.

"Am I dead?"

"No, honey," softly sighs Dad.

***

I feel strong arms encircling me, squeezing. The squeezing starts to become tighter and tighter to the point of pain. "Hey, Dad, you're squeezing the life out of me!" I croak.

"Keep the compressions going!" a strange voice orders. "Where is that crash cart? Breathe, Cathy! I am not going to lose you, not tonight, not on my watch! Step back! Clear!"

Blinding, searing agony! Darkness. Peacefulness. Weightlessness.

Then

Hunting season, the first one in our new home, was quickly approaching. My brothers had both said, "No!" when Dad asked if they wanted to go. I held my tongue. I knew if I showed any desire to go hunting, Lawrence and Jay would immediately change their minds and would demand to go. I would be left behind. So I waited until such time that Dad and I were alone. As luck would happen, I didn't have to wait long!

"The barn needs sweeping," Dad announced to the three of us. My brothers groaned and I pretended to look busy. I knew that Lawrence would point a finger at me.

"Cathy isn't busy!" offered Lawrence.

So predictable! I chuckled to myself. Out loud I argued, "I am helping Mom!"

"Cathy, you are finished helping me," countered Mom.

"But, Dad," I pointed out, "Lawrence hasn't done any work so far today!" I knew Lawrence would argue and Dad would feel frustrated. I would then offer to help solve the dilemma!

"Dad, there she goes again!" Lawrence hotly argued. "Cathy always does this when she has to do any work!"

I couldn't help but chuckle to myself. I had to keep my smile from showing on my face!

"Lawrence, why do you always want Cathy doing the work? You are as lazy as a pet 'coon!" scolded Dad.

Ah, my cue, I thought. Out loud I said sweetly, "Lawrence, I will sweep the barn." I paused, envisioning my angelic halo glowing above my head. "If you do the dishes after supper!" I saw Dad's and Mom's faces light up; thinking that I was being so nice, so mature. My halo started to tarnish with this unearned, unspoken praise. Lawrence, I knew, hated doing dishes more than any other job!

"Dad, I'll sweep the barn," countered Lawrence.

"Too late, son!" chuckled Dad. "You're on dish detail after supper!"

Dad walked to the door and said, "Cathy, I'll show you what I want swept!"

It worked better than I had thought. I kept the smile off my face as I marveled at my ability to manipulate my brothers. Walking down to the barn, I asked about hunting and whether I could come, since my brothers didn't want to.

"I think you would enjoy hunting," Dad said.

I spent the rest of the afternoon sweeping the barn. Dad showed me how to use the large industrial push broom. I discovered that his technique made sweeping the barn easier as I steadily pushed the grime on the floor closer and closer to the entrance. Once at the entrance, I deftly pushed the dirt out in clouds of dust. By the time I had finished, it was dusk outside. I walked smugly up to the house singing, "I'm going hunting – not my brothers!"

I reached for the back-door handle and quickly opened the door. My brothers' angry words hit me, momentarily gluing my feet inside the doorway. "But, Dad, Cathy is a girl! Hunting is not for girls!" whined my brothers in unison.

"It's not fair! You asked us!" Lawrence's voice reflected his indignation at being duped by his sister.

"I want to go!" grumbled Jay.

"Hunting is only for men, not girls!" Lawrence foolishly repeated.

Hmm, I thought, *methinks my brothers have shot themselves in their collective feet!* I could feel my lips curving up into a smile. My brothers' comments about hunting being only for boys would ally Mom with me. Boys can be so dumb at times! As sweetly and innocently as I could be, I entered the kitchen.

"Boys!" Mom shouted over their din. "Your father asked each of you!" It wasn't often that Mom raised her voice, but when she did, everyone obeyed – unquestioningly. "Your father asked you, Lawrence" – she pointed her index finger at my older brother, who was sulking by the kitchen sink – "and you, too" – her finger, like a laser beam, zeroed on Jay, who sank lower on his chair at the table – "and both of you" – a pause – "said what?"

"No," they said meekly, in unison.

"Yes, that's correct! You are not going hunting this year. If you want to go next year, then remember to say 'yes' when your father asks you!"

I always thought my Mom would have made a great hostage negotiator. I could picture it now. A gunman, desperate to escape, with nothing to lose, is cornered inside a bank. This is the same bank he had attempted, unsuccessfully, to rob minutes earlier. He has a gun, a heavy black 9mm semi-automatic. The gun trembles in his unsteady hand. The gun is pointing at a shivering girl sitting on the floor. She is my age. She is his hostage. The other people in the bank had successfully run out when the alarm went off, taking the would-be bank robber by surprise. He had only been able to catch the girl when he grabbed a handful of her long hair as she had tried to run to safety.

The young man is dressed in torn dirty jeans and a T-shirt that has its sleeves ripped off. His dirty brown hair is short and unevenly cut. He grabs the sitting, crying girl by her hair and pulls her to her feet. He drags her over to the window, her body making a shield for the youth. Her body trembles as silent tears course down her tear-streaked cheeks.

"Give me a car!" the young criminal orders.

"Listen, kid, you know we can't do that!" Mom, the police hostage negotiator, yells through a police bullhorn.

"Oh, yeah?" He menaces the girl in the window. "I'll kill this kid!"

"If you kill her," Mom counters, stressing each word, "then her father will kill you!"

"Oh, sure, her old man is going to kill me! Ha!" he scornfully shouts back. "Is that the best you can do?" His voice drips with mockery.

My Mom orders everyone to clear back. This astonishes the bank robber, who slightly loosens his grip on the girl. "What are you up to? What's going on?" he asks suspiciously.

"Like I said," Mom firmly states, "her father will kill you slowly and very painfully!"

The youth is staring at the small woman dressed in dark pants and low-heeled shoes. She is wearing a blue jacket with POLICE written across its back. She seems to be in charge. The other officers are retreating at her command. His grip on the girl is now more for show than for holding onto his hostage. He senses that his escape is near.

"I am not letting you go unless..." Mom pauses before adding, "you kill your hostage! I will inform her father and I will let him take care of you!"

"Why do you think I would be afraid of her old man?" the youth asks, but his voice begins to lose some of its threatening tone. Fear is edging into his mind.

"Perhaps you haven't heard of Big Claude, aka The Butcher!" Mom calmly informs the criminal. His face begins to pale. He is beginning to feel coldness creeping up his spine.

"However," Mom continues, "I can take your hostage back to her father, Big Claude, and tell him what a respectful criminal you are. I'll tell him that you let her go without any threats as soon as you realized your mistake."

Both hostage negotiator and gunman stare at each other. Silence settles over the scene. "However," Mom breaks the silence as she raises her wrist and pointedly looks at her watch. "It is time for dinner with my family, so I'll give you a five count. After I reach five, then no deal. I'll tell Big Claude how you laughed at him and showed no respect for him. One!

Two!"

"Okay, okay!" the youth yells out. "I give up!" He tosses out his gun and sends his hostage out. He follows behind her, raising his hands high above his head.

Police swarm the gunman, grabbing his hands, forcing him down to the pavement, and swiftly pulling his arms behind his back. Handcuffs quickly click into place. Once secured, the youth is pulled up by his arms.

Sandwiched between two police officers, they begin to walk him toward the waiting squad car. He turns towards the negotiator and shouts, "Remember, tell Big Claude I showed respect!"

"Big Claude!" laughs the officer on his left. "Why would Officer Parker's dog care if you showed respect?"

"Cathy!" Mom's voice shattered my daydream. "Are you going to clean up for supper or are you planning to stand there in the doorway like a potted plant?"

My brothers, happy that Mom's attention was no longer directed at them, snickered as I hurried into the utility room to change my clothes and wash up for supper.

***

A couple of weeks later, Dad came home with two hunting licenses. He handed one to me. I looked at my hunting license, the very first one I ever had. "You look after that, Cathy," Dad told me, "because when you bag your deer, we'll attach this to it." The phone rang, interrupting our discussion.

"Who can that be?" Mom queried, as Dad went to answer the phone.

"Hello," Dad said. "Speaking." Dad continued to listen, then said, "Cathy and I." He paused. "No, not the boys. I wanted to take Cathy this time." Instantly I knew Dad was talking to someone about hunting.

"Tomorrow morning, sunrise, okay. Bye." Dad hung up the telephone, turned around and offered, "That was Floyd." Dad looked at Mom. "He phoned to see if we wanted to go deer hunting together. I said sure." Dad held Mom's gaze, assuring her that it'd be safe. I knew they were thinking about last August's community dance, the night's terror, their survival.

"Elizabeth," Dad continued, using the more formal name for my mother, "Floyd was really surprised that Lawrence and Jay weren't going. He said that hunting is just for men!" I looked at Mom and saw her eyes flicker with indignation.

"Why am I not surprised to discover that Floyd Moonie is sexist? I am glad you told him that you wanted to take Cathy."

I marveled at Dad's skill in diverting Mom's attention! Dad winked at me as if he had read my thoughts. I smiled back. Perhaps I inherited my shrewdness from Dad?

We were up early the next morning, so early that it was still dark outside. Mom had made breakfast. Bacon was frying and the scrambled eggs were left on low heat to keep warm. Dad was sipping his coffee when I came into the kitchen dressed in my flannel shirt and denim jeans. "Sit down and eat," Dad said. "We'll be going in a half hour."

Excitedly, I ate my breakfast and sipped my juice. My Mom appeared agitated, upset about something. I feared that she was about to cancel my hunting trip. "Frank," Mom said, putting an end to my fears, "you be careful." My parents exchanged a look of fear, of apprehension. Was I really going into something that was dangerous? This was turning out better than any book I had ever read!

Fifty minutes later, we were at the Moonies' farm. Floyd and Horace were coming outside, carrying their rifles. Horace walked over to their old Ford pickup truck and got inside. Floyd came to our truck and put his head through my open window. "Are you ready?" Dad nodded. "Follow my truck." Floyd turned without a word to me and made his way to his vehicle.

We drove out of the Moonies' yard. The sun started to peek over the eastern horizon. "Dad, Mr Moonie has been drinking!" I whispered incredulously.

"Yes," said Dad. "Stay close to me no matter what happens. I don't want you from my side!"

Dad's earnest tone sent a shiver down my spine. "Dad, do you think Mr Moonie might be dangerous?"

Dad shot me a look of surprise – for a moment I feared that I had given away my snooping on their private conversation. "Anyone is dangerous when alcohol is mixed with a firearm." Relief flooded over me as I nodded my understanding. Dad smiled and patted my head like I was a little kid.

"Dad!" I complained.

Dad added, his blue eyes twinkling, "You're always going to be my wee lass no matter how old you get!"

Minutes later, the red lights of the Moonies' old Ford shone brightly. We slowed down, gently braked and stopped behind Floyd's truck. Horace and his father got out of their vehicle; we did the same. We converged together in a conspiratorial party. "I saw a buck and a doe," said Floyd in a hushed voice.

"Where?" asked Dad in an equally hushed voice.

"They went into the bush over there," said Horace, pointing towards a copse of trees about thirty yards southwest from us.

"You kids go through the bush from this side, and we'll drive to the opposite side. Make lots of noise as you go. We will be able to shoot any deer you scare out." Mr Moonie said, looking at us; I was looking at Dad.

"Floyd, since this is Cathy's first-time hunting, I want her to stay with me," Dad said in a friendly tone, but a tone that allowed no further discussion.

"Frank," said Floyd, almost too enthusiastically, "that is a great idea!" Surprised, I stole a glance at Horace. He stood slightly behind his father, and his tension was palpable. Once more I recalled the hushed, scared voices of my parents.

"Horace and I will flush this bush," Floyd declared, "and you and Cathy will get the first crack at bagging a deer. Then we will switch at the next bush. We'll leave my truck here. We'll pick it up later." Floyd promptly turned and ordered Horace to follow him into the bush.

"Get in the truck!" Dad softly urged me, as we hurried back to the truck. I couldn't help feeling that the hushed timbre of Dad's voice was fear as well as a desire not to scare any game away. We slowly began to circle the bush. We stopped when we arrived at a point that was opposite Floyd's expected exit from the bush. We got out and waited. It was not a long wait.

My .25-06 felt heavy in my arms. I positioned myself on an angle from the bush, waiting for a deer to come running out. "Remember, don't fire into the bush. Shoot only if you have a clear shot at the deer. If you are not sure—" started Dad.

"Don't shoot!" I finished with a smile on my lips. We waited hours it seemed, but it was only a few minutes. The noise being made by Floyd and Horace steadily grew louder and louder. Suddenly, a large doe charged out of the bush and came to a complete stop twenty feet from us! I carefully raised my rifle as I had done when I was target shooting. I took aim, breathed in, breathed out and gently pulled the trigger.

The rifle gave a gentle kick, but its sound was like a drum being struck right beside my ear! The doe stood her ground and began to eat! Did she not realize that I was about to kill her? I guess not. The second and third shots brought about the same lack of response from the deer. Was she deaf, I wondered to myself? Just as quickly, I remembered that Floyd and Horace had scared her out of the bush with noise. I sighed. I aimed for the fourth time and fired.

The doe slowly turned her head towards me and stared at me with milk-chocolate eyes as if it was saying, 'Is that the best you can do? You want me to run away for this? Well, I'm leaving, but I'm leaving because I am bored with your feeble attempts to frighten me!'

The deer slowly turned her head to look straight ahead and calmly started to saunter off, taunting me to shoot. I took aim for the last time. I shot. The bullet struck the ground, throwing dirt onto her hind legs. Surprised, she leapt into the air and was off! Floyd and Horace came crashing out of the bush in time to see the deer disappearing over the distant ridgeline.

"Frank, how could you have missed that deer?" asked Floyd, his irritation evident in the early dawn.

"I missed," I said meekly.

"You!" Floyd yelled. "Frank, you let her, a girl, shoot at a deer and miss? Why didn't you shoot it for her?"

"Because," Dad said, anger simmering in his voice, "it was her animal. The next one is yours, Floyd."

"Humph!" Floyd said. "Let's go to the next bush!"

We walked silently back to our truck. Floyd and Horace climbed into the truck box. We climbed into the cab. Floyd slapped the truck's roof and Dad rolled down the window on his door. "Frank, drive around the other side; stop if you see a deer still sleeping. It'll be a sure kill!" yelled Floyd, his voice sounding as if he was inside our truck cab.

"Dad, we can't kill a deer while it is asleep! That isn't fair!" I said in hushed tones.

"Shh!" Dad said in a loud whisper, then softly added, "I'll try to scare it awake. I hope we don't see one, that's all!"

We started to slowly circle the bush. I felt that any moment we would discover a helpless deer asleep. Tension was tightening its grip on our small group. Dad, without warning, leaned on the horn! The noise was deafening! I jumped in alarm; glad I was seatbelted in! Without the tightening of the seatbelt, I would have hit the roof with my head.

"Frank! Frank!" Floyd yelled, and slammed his fist against the roof of the cab. "Have you gone crazy? You're going to scare every deer for miles!"

As he continued to slowly ease the truck around another bush, Dad quit honking and yelled back, "Exactly! I should scare something up, then we will have one to shoot!" Suddenly, I understood Dad's true motive. What deer could possibly sleep through that noise? I smiled at Dad in appreciation; Dad gave me a conspiratorial wink in return.

We spent the better part of the morning circling bush after bush, honking and looking. We took turns riding in the truck box. Whoever was riding in the truck box had the right to get down and to shoot. No one was permitted to fire from the cab or from the back of the truck. The morning was lengthening, and I remained the only hunter who had shot at a deer. Floyd continued to lament over that fact, restating that my Dad should have shot and killed the deer. It didn't seem to matter to Floyd that it was promised to me.

We had just switched positions – Dad and I were seated inside of our pickup, Floyd and Horace outside in the box – when Dad's honking scared up a deer! Momentarily, I thought it was my doe with the chocolate eyes. I secretly hoped it wasn't. "Stop!" commanded Floyd. Before the truck came to a complete halt, Floyd and Horace had jumped out of the truck box.

Hurriedly, they crouched in the long grass. Floyd was just behind and to Horace's left. The deer was upwind and didn't smell the two hunters aiming their rifles at it. I saw Floyd nudge Horace, who shuddered instinctively. I realized that Horace was to make the kill. I also knew that Horace was as surprised as I was when his father nudged him. I silently prayed that he would be successful, as I feared how Floyd would react if he missed. I had seconds to think these thoughts as Horace raised his rifle, aimed, and fired.

I heard two shots and thought how strange for an echo to sound so close to the originating shot. Horace's face turned from surprise to pallid. Regret showed over his young face. I understood then that he had intentionally tried to miss the deer. "Way to go, boy!" shouted Floyd, who jumped up from behind Horace and slapped him on his back. Horace and I instantaneously realized that Floyd had killed the deer Horace had purposefully missed! Floyd had positioned himself behind his son, possibly anticipating that Horace would miss, an action Floyd would not accept from his son.

We approached the fallen deer. Dad touched my arm and cautioned, "Stand well back from its hooves, Cathy."

"That's right, little girl," smugly added Floyd. "I've seen deer lash out with those sharp hooves and cut a man's leg wide open!"

I looked at Dad, who nodded. We positioned ourselves to the front of the doe's head. Unexpectedly, the deer opened its eyes and began to cry out in anguish! Momentarily, I thought Floyd had shot a baby. I stumbled back away from the doe.

"Cut its throat!" commanded Floyd, handing a large deadly looking Ka-bar Becker Moses Bowie knife to Horace. Horace took the sixteen-inch black knife in a trembling hand. His eyes reflected the misery I saw in the doe's eyes. "What are you waiting for? Cut its throat so it'll bleed properly!" Floyd yelled.

Horace seemed to be rooted to the ground. He was looking overwhelmed with the imminent death of this beautiful animal sounding so much like a baby. Tears welled up in my eyes. Floyd roughly grabbed Horace's hand that held the knife and pulled Horace towards the wounded deer. Three steps and Floyd pushed Horace down on his knees. Kneeling beside Horace, Floyd stiffened his grip on his boy's hand and slit open the doe's throat. The sounds of a baby crying ended abruptly in a spray of hot, steaming arterial blood. The doe lay unmoving on the ground in a pool of blood, its throat slit straight across. In disgust, I turned and walked back to our truck, vowing never to hunt again. The feeling of revulsion was powerful, but not as great as my repugnance of Floyd and his treatment of Horace.

Now

"Don't cry," a comforting voice soothes me.

"Dad? Is that you? Where are you?" I whisper into the darkness around me.

I hear someone chuckling. I hear words from my long-ago childhood. "Lass, you know it's me. I'm here and I'll always be here for you."

I look to my left and I see Dad sitting beside me on the wooden dock. Our feet are dangling over the edge. Dad puts his arm around me and hugs me tightly to his side.

"I have missed you, Cathy!" Dad's voice is full of tenderness.

"Am I dead?" *Duh, yes*, my inquisitive rational voice answers my query. Yep, of course I'd have to keep that sarcastic voice even in the afterlife!

"No, well, not actually," Dad starts. "You have to decide if you want to stay," he finishes somewhat clumsily.

"Yes! I want to stay with you, Dad! I have missed you so much!" I hug him back. I know that this is where I want to remain, forever.

***

Bright light abruptly shines into my eyes, blinding me. "Her heartbeat is falling. I need 5mg of epinephrine. STAT. Come on, Cathy, come back, damn it!"

"We've got her rhythm back," a disjointed voice flutters down like snowflakes on a winter night.

"Dad." But no sound is heard. Dad is gone. His strong arm around my shoulders is gone, too. "Dad," I moan.

Darkness. Loneliness. Tears start flowing.

***

Clanging of dishes, squeaking shoes on polished floors, hushed voices, my eyes try to open, but my eyelids seem to be glued shut. I try to move – pain shoots through my head, making me see stars. A moan emanates from my closed lips.

"I'm sorry, dear," says a soothing, disembodied voice. "I was busy in Room 1015 and now I am running a little late with your pain medicine." Rustling of clothes, clinking of tubes against metal. "There – you should start feeling better soon. Another day and you'll be off the fentanyl. But don't worry, we have other pain meds. You just rest, dear, and return to us. It isn't your time to go."

Peacefulness. Blackness. Weightlessness.

Then

I attended the U of R in Regina and graduated four years later with a degree in journalism. This was to be the first half of my career as an investigative reporter. My other half, I decided, should be in law enforcement. I enrolled in the Royal Canadian Mounted Police academy in Regina.

I had successfully completed three hundred eighty-two hours of training, and I was just entering the one hundred four 'Firearms' hours in my cadet training program. I worked and trained harder than I ever did during my four years at university. Exhausted, each day I fell asleep punctually at twenty-two hundred hours and I didn't stir until zero six hundred hours.

The persistent chirping of my cell phone woke me up after a particularly grueling day on the firing range. Groggily, I noticed several missed calls, all from my Mom. "Oh, man," I groaned, "it's not even five!" My mother was doggedly calling me over and over. I fumbled the phone, croaking, "Hi, Mom."

The words Mom spoke over my mobile phone instantly disintegrated my life, my family. "Finally, Cathy!" Mom's voice seemed terse. I was about to say that I was working very hard in my training, and I needed my sleep, but Mom continued to talk as if she was reading a script. "Dad suffered a massive heart attack…" Heart-wrenching sobbing stopped Mom's words for a few minutes. When I thought no more words were coming, Mom sobbed, "I took his lunch to the field…" Her crying again stopped her words. "Cathy, the doctors told me to notify the family." The silence was broken by muffled crying. "I tried to get you last night, but you weren't answering."

"Mom," I said, tears flowing out of my eyes, "I am on my way! Which hospital is Dad in?"

Mom continued as if she had not heard me. She was repeating the words she had said to Lawrence and again to Jay. "I found Frank lying on the ground beside the air seeder." Mom was crying so hard, I was afraid she would hang up before I knew where Dad was.

"Which hospital?" I asked again, panic escalating. "Mom?" All I could hear was heart-wrenching sobs from my mother, who is the toughest person I know!

"The doctors told me to phone the kids. They don't think Frank will make the day!"

"Mom, I am coming! Which hospital?" We were both sobbing.

"Come to the Royal University Hospital." The phone went dead.

I threw a few things into my backpack and left my one-bedroom apartment. As I ran down the stairs, I phoned the RCMP depot to report my absence for the next week due to a family emergency.

I drove the two-and-a-half-hours to Saskatoon Royal University Hospital in well under two hours. I absently thought that it would not look good if I was pulled over for speeding, but the words that Dad might not live through today propelled me like a rocket down the Louis Riel Trail to Saskatoon. I was thankful to Fate or to God, or whatever was at work during my heart-breaking, sobbing drive to Saskatoon, that I didn't meet up with either stray wildlife or an RCMP constable on highway patrol.

True to Mom's dire words, I lost Dad twelve hours after I received that hateful, cruel call.

The next few days passed by in a blur of well-wishers, visits to Fotheringham's Funeral Home to finalize arrangements, and finally the funeral itself.

Unbeknown to me, my parents had bought two plots in a small cemetery on the east side of Saskatoon. My parents thought that it summed up their lives: the move East to farm and the train tracks (our life in Purple Springs with trains passing through town several times a day). The somber procession of vehicles, led by the gray hearse and limousine, parked in the ample parking lot by Green Acres Cemetery. People moved slowly from their vehicles to the newly dug graveside to stand quietly.

Horace walked up to me after the graveside service and took me into his arms. His body felt good. "Cathy…" His voice was husky with emotion. "I loved your Dad! I can't believe he's gone!"

I looked up into his red-rimmed eyes and replied, "Neither can I! I always thought I would have more time to spend with Dad after I finished with school!"

We stood there, looking at Dad's bronze casket with four red roses scattered on its lid. Soft voices wafted over, like a lullaby soothing my emotions. People slowly made their way back to the many parked vehicles.

"I have to go," I whispered when I saw the driver standing beside the gray limousine waiting for me. "I hope you will come back to the church and have lunch."

"If you want me to," Horace replied. He looked ill at ease.

I took his hand and noticed how warm it felt in my cold hand. "Of course I do! But I must go. Thank you for coming, if I don't see you later." I turned and quickly walked to the waiting limousine and my family less one.

Tears trickled out of my eyes.

I sat at our small table and dispassionately watched as people approached and hugged my Mom over and over. Many neighbors assured my Mom that her crops would be sown and harvested in the fall. Offers of condolences were spoken to my brothers and me. I sat mute. I couldn't bring the simple words 'thank you' to my lips. My brothers softly talked between themselves.

Their concern centered on how they could take care of Mom. Lawrence thought Mom should move into a condo. Jay suggested an apartment complex for seniors. They continued discussing the advantages of both.

"Cathy," a husky voice broke me out of my detachment from the people around me. I looked up into Horace's blue gray eyes that were bloodshot from crying. His face was also flushed.

"Horace," I said, standing up to hug him. "I am glad you were able to have something to eat."

"Cathy, can we go outside to talk? It is a little hot in here." His voice was soft and husky.

Smiling, I took his offered hand and we walked out into a glorious day to everyone but me. I felt hollowed out.

"I wanted to congratulate you on your graduation from university. Your dad was so proud of you!"

More tears threatened, but I swiped them away, saying, "I can't seem to quit crying!"

"It will get easier," Horace softly said, his eyes trying to absorb my pain. "Would you like to join me for dinner, unless you're planning to return to Regina?"

"Yes, I'd love to! I'm staying at the Hampton Inn, so I won't be heading back until tomorrow. I will have to check with Mom and see what her plans are. I don't want to leave her alone tonight."

Horace pulled me into his arms and hugged me tightly. "Your Mom is going out with your brothers."

I pulled back, surprised. "Really? Why wasn't I invited?" My voice reflected the hurt I was feeling at being excluded.

Horace smiled, saying, "I am afraid that I am responsible!" As I looked more confused with his words, he continued, "I told them that since they wanted to discuss moving your mother either into a condo or an apartment, something I know you are not in favor of, it would work better if you were not included in this initial conversation!" His blue gray eyes twinkled with mischief.

"Horace, you are so devious!" I said, laughing. "You know Mom would not do anything without me being involved! Thank you. I need a night away from the pain."

"I will pick you up at seven?"

"That will work for me. I must get back," I softly said. I reached up and gently hugged him, whispering, "Thank you."

Several hours later, after we were finishing our delicious meals at the Red Lobster, my daydream of Horace and me finally becoming serious was shattered when Horace asked, "What are your plans now that you are finished with school?"

"Well, I am not finished with school yet," I smiled, unsure of my future that only last month seemed so clear.

"Oh, yeah, your Dad was saying that you were looking at another course, but I believe it wasn't definite when he and I spoke last."

"That was because I had to be accepted!" I smiled, trying to sound mysterious.

"Accepted? Into what?"

"I am enrolled in the RCMP cadet program at the depot in Regina!" Pride was evident in my voice. Horace looked at me, but no words were forthcoming. Horace's face drained of all colour. Puzzled at his reaction, I tried to smile. I asked, "What's the matter?"

Horace forced back the kindness that I saw moments earlier, but this time it failed to reach his eyes. "All the best, Cathy, in this new endeavor." Horace's voice was impassionate. His eyes were distant.

"Horace," I hesitantly started, "I thought..." But my voice faltered.

"Cathy, I don't want to step in the way of your dream!" Horace said indifferently. Horace signaled our waiter and asked for the bill.

Stunned at the abrupt ending of our evening together, I mutely watched as Horace paid for our meals. He added, "It is getting late, and I must drive back home tonight. I still have another seven hundred acres to plant."

When Horace and I pulled up at the Hampton Inn in his Dodge Ram, he broke the silence of the drive by saying, "I am going to miss your Dad." Horace leant over the console and gave me a brotherly hug with a kiss placed lightly on my cheek.

"Me, too," I murmured as I got out of his dark blue truck. I stood at the hotel entrance doors, my heart aching as I looked at his receding truck. Horace had always been there, but now I somehow knew he was leaving me. What had happened that turned him from a loving friend to just another neighbor?

Tears fell once more, but this time my tears were for losing Horace as abruptly as losing my Dad.

***

Back in Regina, during the firearms course, I made a discovery about myself. I realized that I didn't have what it took to shoot any person; it was unthinkable to me. I knew that I could not shoot a person even if I was in a life and death situation. I quit shortly after. Within a year, I experienced the death of my career as an RCMP constable, the death of my Dad and the death of my one-sided platonic relationship with Horace.

You know, my antagonistic inner voice pointed out, *bad luck always comes in threes!* I countered that I must be in store for some good luck!

Buoyed up, I began my job search as a reporter. One afternoon, shortly after I dropped out of the cadet training program, Susan, a friend from university, invited me to come for coffee at our favorite local café. While drinking coffee, black for both of us, Susan told me about a position as a trial reporter at the *Wheatland Daily Press* in Saskatoon. Susan wasn't interested in applying for this position because her fiancé was working in Regina, and he was not willing to quit his job and move to Saskatoon. Susan urged me to apply and I agreed! We toasted her fiancé's unwillingness to move and my good fortune! We clinked our coffee cups. To complete our celebration, we ordered a chocolate-dipped donut for each of us!

I applied that night. I fell asleep thinking that I needed to move out of Regina. It had too many bad memories. I decided that I'd move to Saskatoon and look for work even if this job opening didn't work for me.

Later that week, I received a text message from a Saskatoon number asking if I would drive to the *Wheatland Daily Press* to come in for an interview. I quickly texted 'yes' and asked for the details.

Early the next morning, I found myself driving on the same highway that only a short time ago I had driven in fear of losing my Dad. Today, I drove the almost three-hour journey to Saskatoon without pleading and bargaining with God. I decided that after the interview I would find a place to rent, then I would move to Saskatoon, to either work at the

Wheatland Daily Press or to find a job at another news outlet. This decision calmed my nerves as I drove to my first interview since quitting my course at the RCMP academy.

I left the *Wheatland Press* building emotionally drained. I hadn't counted on my raw memories of losing Dad, reconnecting with Horace, then just as abruptly losing him, and then quitting my training to become an RCMP officer to affect me so strongly during my interview. They must have thought that I was a brick short of a load! I believed my interview was a disaster – even I wouldn't hire me! Had I torpedoed my first chance at being a reporter? I vowed that I'd be better prepared next time as I pulled up to the Hampton Inn. I suddenly realized that I had stayed here when I rushed to be with my Dad for the last time!

I changed into my workout clothes. I needed to purge my feelings of despair, hurt and frustration with the weights and treadmill that were for use by the guests of the Hampton Inn. As I reached for the door to the fitness center, my phone rang. I answered it and Lou Klassen, from the *Wheatland Daily Press*, said in his no-nonsense voice, "I think you will be a good fit for the *Wheatland Daily Press*. If you feel the same, then I'd like to welcome you to our newspaper."

"Thank you, Mr Klassen!"

"Cathy, it is Lou if you want to stay on my good side!"

Immediately, I forgot the fitness center. I stopped by the front desk and extended my stay for another couple of days. I picked up a local real estate paper to take back to my room, where I started to look for my new home to go with my new job!

***

Many people in the Saskatoon area could tell you about a great reporter: Robin McCathy at the *Wheatland Daily Press*. If you'd asked them, they would describe Robin's writing technique, his various reports published in the paper, along with his opinions on different judgments and sentences passed onto the local criminal element. But the public did not know anything about the personal side of Saskatoon's popular reporter.

Robin McCathy was invisible to the public; only his forceful writing was visible, along with his thought-provoking commentary. Who was Robin McCathy? Robin McCathy was me, Cathy Parker!

I used this pseudonym to ensure that I would have the freedom to report in-depth the various crimes that appeared in Provincial Court. This would not be possible if my identity was known, because even today, in the twenty-first century, women are not always taken seriously in journalism! I also thought it would be safer when I finally got into investigative reporting, my professional goal. I had started my campaign over the last few years with my editor, Lou Klassen, to let me start in this field, but without success. Mom didn't know what my true job was at the *Wheatland Daily Press*.

If I was asked, I would not be able to say why I didn't share my secret with Mom. Perhaps I was waiting until I really was an investigative reporter.

Instead, I told Mom and my brothers that I took the position of an administrative assistant until I could find something better. Mom had slowly come to terms that I was wasting my life and my bachelor's degree in journalism working at the *Wheatland Daily Press* as a secretary!

Lou, my boss, had a problem with women investigative reporters – he believed that women were genetically incapable of investigative reporting. In Lou's mind, it was remarkable that women could report more than the newest fashions, bake sales and child-rearing stories! Women, according to Lou, were too sensitive, too fragile, and too delicate to go into potentially dangerous situations and investigate newsworthy news! I was seriously contemplating moving to another newspaper, when Geoff O'Connor was hired as *Wheatland*'s newest investigative reporter. Geoff became Lou's favorite investigative reporter. He was also able to worm his way into my heart as I slowly developed a platonic infatuation with him!

Aren't you getting a little old to have a crush on a guy? Granted, my own thoughts were often very snide, but what can a person do? I had to admit that I was feeling helpless to stop fantasizing after Geoff, and age had nothing to do with this.

Geoff O'Connor was the first man in years to make me feel like a woman. I admired him for his looks, for his reporting skills, as well as for his investigative ability. It seemed that throughout my whole life platonic love was what I excelled at. My Dad had often told me that I set my standards too high, to which I would reply that I would rather be single than to lower my standards just to be married. Such words uttered when I was young and hopeful became sadder and more hopeless as I aged. These were my somber feelings on my fortieth birthday, when Geoff changed my life forever.

"Morning, Cathy," was Geoff's usual greeting each morning. My body tingled whenever I heard him say these two simple words to me. His voice resonated deep inside of his chest as it tingled my synapses. I must admit it was the sexiest voice I had heard, well, in a very long time.

Today was different as he continued talking. "And happy birthday, too!"

"How did you know?" I asked, feeling my face flush. My birthday was not something I advertised. I preferred to ignore this yearly reminder that time was ticking away. That my life was stalled at the STARTING line.

"I am an investigative reporter! I investigated, of course!" Geoff chuckled. "How would you like to celebrate the big four-oh? I was thinking supper at the O.K. Corral?"

I stood there at a loss for words. If only my readers could see the great Robin McCathy speechless! I stood looking up into his intelligent steel blue eyes. Eyes that seemed to reach out and wrap me in his arms!

I had not realized that I was still staring at him when Geoff added, "Well, er, that is if you hadn't already made plans." I never thought I'd bear witness to Geoff feeling unsure of himself! His brow was marred with a frown.

"Oh, no, actually I hadn't thought about doing anything special for my birthday," I stammered. "Thanks, Geoff, I would love to celebrate my birthday with you!" I finished awkwardly. Why did I always feel so inept whenever I exchanged words with any man I was attracted to?

"Great!" said Geoff, his characteristic confidence replacing his momentary insecurity. "I will come by at six thirty, if that works for you?"

"Six thirty, great!" I said, thinking that I was going to have to leave punctually at five, something I usually did not do. "That should give me time to get ready after work," I finished lamely.

"You look great just as you are!" Geoff offered. What emotion was I seeing in his eyes? Friendship? Kindness? Helping a lonely woman? Or was it something more? *Get real!* my inner voice scolded me. *Here you are, already jumping into bed with the man! He just asked you if you wanted to go out for your birthday, not to have his babies!* Okay, maybe the baby part was a bit over the top, but I had to begrudgingly admit my inner voice did make a valid argument! My first date in several years was set: I was going out with a man whom I had lusted over in my dreams while envying his being able to investigate crime – where the real action was!

Geoff was five feet eleven inches tall, but he seemed taller, perhaps due to the way he walked, his head held high, his shoulders squared back and his chest out. Geoff's dark brown hair was independent of his calm exterior. His hair had its own personal unfelt wind that kept the thick dark waves crashing into one another. The patches of gray hair looked like whitecaps on rough water. Geoff, at forty-four, exuded the confidence of successful men in their personal fields of expertise. Geoffrey Thomas O'Connor was built like a fullback, moved like a bear, but with the grace of Fred

Astaire. Muhammad Ali's words, "floats like a butterfly" came to mind whenever I saw Geoff walking.

***

I decided to wear my pull-on camel slacks with my French blue cotton shirt. I added my gold chain to peek out from the open neck of my shirt. I checked my image in the full-length mirror. Statue, somewhat short at five feet one, bust too large, waist should be smaller, stomach too rounded, and, taking two steps closer to the mirror, I discovered even more facial lines. "Cheerfulness or age?" I asked my mirror image. "Cheerfulness," I smiled at my mirror image. My subsequent smiling created a myriad of lines. "If you never smiled," I sagely counselled my reflection, "you would not have wrinkles!"

I could hear Mom admonishing me: *Cathy, if you took care of your face, you would have less wrinkles!* "All right, mother," I said resignedly, "what cream do you want me to use?" I went into my bathroom and opened my vanity. Creams, creams, and more creams stared out at me! Each cream promised less wrinkles than the others. "Which of you will perform a miracle and make my wrinkles disappear?" I softly asked my silent staring audience of colorful jars. I studied them quietly; no advising voice answered. I closed my eyes and chose one. I opened my eyes to see a blue bottle of cream in my hand. "Umm, good choice, hand," I congratulated myself. Then, just as quick, I think, *What is Geoff going to think, you talking to yourself; and worse, to your jars of creams!* Good point. Time to act like an adult.

I straightened my shoulders and adeptly massaged the chosen cream into my face.

I put on my diamond earrings, the one luxury that I had bought for myself. Diamonds represent eternity. But what eternity? Did I need an eternity to find love? Or an eternity of being in love? *Being in love with a real man and not your various platonic loves!* Yes, my inner voice was in fine form tonight. I just hoped that the evening was going to be half as great as I had created in my many romantic fantasies of Geoff. *Shh*, I admonished my inner voice as I sensed another cynical comment percolating up to be shared.

The ringing of the doorbell successfully stopped any more thoughts, welcomed or unbidden, to infiltrate my mind. I checked myself once more in the mirror and quickly walked to the door. I opened the door to Geoff, standing in my doorway. He looked younger, dressed in a Panhandle blue Aztec Western shirt tucked into his beltless blue jeans. To complete his ensemble was a pair of brown Ariat heritage dress cowboy boots. In his left hand he held a red long-stem rose, which he handed to me. "Thank you!" I said, suddenly feeling completely foolish and awkward. How do women, normal women, do this?

Perhaps Geoff noticed my reaction or lack of reaction. "I wanted to give you one red rose as a way of telling you that I plan to" – here Geoff stumbled over his planned words – "would like to add more roses to create a bouquet."

I put the rose into my slender single flower cut crystal vase and poured water into it from the kitchen faucet. I sat it on my kitchen counter. Turning back to Geoff and smiling, I said, "So this rose could be considered as a down payment of sorts?" My smile grew as I took pleasure flustering the paper's newest investigative reporter. Was it possible he was feeling as awkward as I was feeling?

Before I could continue to muse over this, Geoff stopped my thoughts with his next words. "Yes! Next time I'll spring for two roses!" Geoff chuckled.

"Be still my heart!" I said, putting my hand over my heart, adding, "Perhaps if I have enough birthdays, I might envision receiving a dozen long-stem roses!"

Laughing, we left for dinner. *Why so nervous? You work with him and you have done so for the past two years. Quit acting like he's a blind date!* My inner voice nailed it perfectly. Sighing, I began to relax. Geoff reached out and took my hand, engulfing it with his large hand, and smiled down at me, asking, "Why the sigh?"

Laughing, I said, "I was acting like you're a blind date and not someone I have worked with every day for the last two years! We're both reporters working for the same company. I am going to relax!"

"What, you're a reporter," he chuckled, "not an administrative assistant?"

"Yes," I admonished playfully, "so everything you say will be on the record!"

"I thought the only other reporters on staff were men. Hey, wait, one reporter did catch my eye. Let me think." Geoff paused, a smile spreading across his face, lighting up his eyes. "I believe his name is Robin McCathy! I knew there was something different with that reporter!"

Laughing playfully, I quipped, "Only you and a select few know my writer's identity! Tonight, you'll have to content yourself to be out with Cathy Parker, an administrative assistant!" Deep down, I enjoyed using my *nom de plume*, Robin McCathy. I equally enjoyed people praising his abilities as a courtroom reporter.

Geoff and I drove out to a quiet dining spot ten kilometers east of Saskatoon. The O.K. Corral was a newly opened restaurant set back in the 1800s. The O.K. Corral's reviews were glowing as it continued to draw people in to experience some Western history. I had been planning on going myself, so I was doubly pleased that Geoff had chosen this spot.

"I thought that it would be nice to come here," Geoff said as he pulled into the parking lot. "I thought that a birthday celebration of the big four-oh would be more special if we went to a new, never-before-experienced place!" Geoff paused, as if a thought had just struck him. "You haven't been here before, have you?"

He looked so innocent and so eager to please me that I was instantly irrationally happy that I could honestly say, "I've never been here before! What an incredibly thoughtful birthday present, even if it must be for my big four-oh!"

The parking lot did not resemble anything I was familiar with. Rows of old-fashioned hitching posts marked parking spaces for the O.K. Corral's customers. There were no horses to be hitched, but only parked vehicles of different types, shapes and colors. Mechanical horses waiting for their owners to come and drive them home! Horses that did not need water troughs to drink from or feed bags to be put over their heads!

The parking lot seemed full! My dream date was beginning to deflate.

Geoff didn't seem worried; in fact, he appeared to have a definite destination. He drove down a second row of hitched, mechanical horses, when he expertly pulled into an empty space. Geoff got out and removed a sign that had been shoved through a hand-wrought-iron nail. On it, the words 'Reserved for Geoff O'Connor' were printed in Viner Hand italic font on artificially aged, yellowed paper.

Smiling, Geoff walked around the front of his dark green second-hand Ford Escape to open my door. He held out his hand to me, which I took, while saying in my best Scarlett O'Hara southern accent, "Why, thank you, kind sir." I sent up an apology to *Gone with The Wind*'s Scarlett O'Hara for my poor imitation.

The O.K. Corral stood before us; a huge rambling ranch house built in the style of the 1800s. Its mixture of logs and stones added to its rustic Western charm. Glowing kerosene lamps could be seen through the many small windows. "It looks like a full house tonight," I remarked.

"That's why I made a reservation," Geoff chuckled. "Most nights are like this. Come, let's go inside and enjoy dinner!"

Hand in hand, we walked the last several yards to the O.K. Corral. We lightly climbed the three very wide, very long wooden steps that led up to an old, heavy-looking door. Its aged timber planks also had hand-wrought-iron nails pounded into them, leaving their uneven heads protruding from the wood. Situated about halfway down the right side of the door was a tarnished metal bridge door pull. Geoff grabbed and pulled on it, opening the door for me. "I am not used to men opening doors for me," I said, my face feeling hot and flushed. Incompetence flooded into me. I felt more like a teenager on her first date than a forty-year-old woman!

"I will always open any and all doors for you, Cathy," Geoff said, suddenly very seriously. My heart sped up. Whoa there, heart! You are not a teenager; you are a woman pushing middle age! My heart was soundly scolded by my very blunt self. Yeah, but a middle-aged woman feeling very young, attractive, and yes, sexy, countered my heart! I smiled as I thought that Geoff would be running away screaming if he knew I regularly argued with my opposing voices, often losing to one or the other! I noticed Geoff was returning the smile.

Slowly, so very slowly, a memory from decades ago swam up to the surface of my consciousness. Another young man had entered my life and I dreamt of marriage, kids, happily ever after. Horace's face slowly came into focus, frozen as a youth forever in time.

"Cathy, I know I have a handsome face, great eyes and a magnetic personality, but I can't read your mind!" Geoff's gentle voice intruded on my thoughts.

"Oh, I am sorry," I stammered. "I was just thinking how long I had wanted to go out with you!" I said, my face flushing with my partial lie.

"Me, too!" Geoff laughed. His laughter was hearty, coming from deep down in his chest. "But I am hungry, so do you think we can order first, and then share our daydreams about each other later?"

The host, dressed in Western finery from the late 1800s, introduced himself. "Virgil Earp here. Please follow me." He wove his way through tables that accommodated couples talking in hushed, intimate voices. One table had a group of eight people talking and laughing loudly, no intimacy there. He finally stopped at a table for two that was at a right angle to the huge stone fireplace. The fireplace was made of large river rocks. The live edge mantel was wide enough for a person to lay down on it! It was five feet in length and was centered perfectly on the fireplace. The large fire, behind a steel mesh grate, was warm and inviting.

Geoff pulled out my chair and I thanked him. We took the menus our host gave us. He departed, saying that he would be around soon to take our order. "That is strange," I murmured so as to not be overheard by the departing Virgil, "the host usually doesn't wait tables."

"Here the host or hostess is the personal server for his or her reservation," Geoff replied. "That is why this place is so popular! You get personal service from the moment you park!"

"Well, I hope they give your mechanical horse some water and maybe some oats to eat!" Laughing, we took to reading the menu, which also added to the Western atmosphere of the O.K. Corral. Formatted like a wanted dead or alive poster, the words 'Wanted Hot and Tasty' were printed in extra-large black Viner Hand italic letters at the top of the menu. Along the right side of the menu were pictures of the entrées, and across from each picture was its corresponding name, followed by the reward for each. Quickly, I realized this was the cost of each item.

Our host, as if he knew we were ready to order, returned to our table.

Keeping in character and tipping his white felt cowboy hat, he said, "Howdy, ma'am! Sir! Which of them hombres do you want me to round up for y'all tonight?"

"First," I said, smiling, "would you be related to Wyatt Earp?"

"Why, ma'am, he's my brother," he replied. "Would you like to guess how many brothers I have?"

"Four," Geoff and I said together.

Chuckling, he added, "Yep, and we love to tease and torment our two sisters!"

My stomach growled, reddening my face. "I will take the flaming beef kabob."

"Make that two flaming beef kabobs!" Geoff added. "Also bring a bottle of Red Zinfandel wine, please."

"Very well, sir," Virgil said, and left our table.

We spent the next few minutes admiring the architecture of the interior of the O.K. Corral and its authenticity to the 1800s. Our conversation slowly turned serious when Geoff asked, "Do you believe in fate, in love at first sight?"

I took his hand into mine. 'Yes' was ready to jump out of my mouth, just as our very efficient waiter chose this moment to return with the wine.

Virgil expertly opened the bottle of wine with a 'pop!' when the cork was pulled from the bottle. The sound, disturbingly like a gunshot, took me back in time, seeing once more those chocolate eyes helplessly looking at me as Floyd's hand encased Horace's smaller hand, and together, they cut the deer's throat.

Now

I look around. My limbs are translucent. My hands, too.
How can this be? Why do I not feel afraid? Why do I feel
loved? Why do I not worry about being here in a flowing
white robe made of material that I cannot feel? I realize that
I am standing in a field filled with flowers, hundreds of
beautiful flowers, all brilliantly shining, their petals
composed of vibrant colors I've never seen on Earth! The
flowers are gently swaying back and forth in a breeze, but a
breeze I can't feel! So strange and yet so peaceful. I pull
my gaze from the flowers to look around and, unsurprisingly,
I see my Dad! Dad waves and calls to me!

Instantly, without the necessity of movement, I am
standing beside him. "Dad, why are we here?"

"Honey, what I am going to tell you is important." Dad's
words are spoken with the seriousness of that long-ago night
when he was offering me advice before I went out on my first
date. "I want you to remember. Your past is your present and
your future." My Dad's voice is very solemn as he speaks
these words.

"Now you're sounding like a fortune cookie!" I laugh
uncomfortably. I put my arms up to hug him, but he is fading,
the field is fading, I'm fading.

Suddenly, unseen hands grab me. They tightly seize my shoulders, my arms, my legs and start to spin me around.

"What the—?" I start to say when the spinning speeds up, faster and faster. My body tilts over. I start falling headfirst into what? Terror takes hold of me as I tumble faster and faster. I fight for purchase, but there is nothing to grab on to. Darkness envelops me. In terror, I scream and thrash, but still I continue to drop like a boulder, faster and faster.

***

Unexpectedly, I feel different strong hands grab me abruptly, stopping this terrifying headlong spiraling fall into eternity. "Shh," a soft, tender voice says, "you're safe now. We have you."

Shuddering with relief, I relax as I feel warmth wrapping around me. "Thank you," I murmur, but did I say it out loud?

***

I open my eyes and I see that I am once more standing in a beautiful sunny meadow. I look around, and this time I see mountains off on the horizon. I look down and see plants, beautiful, colorful plants, but plants that I have never seen before. Plants I am sure are not found on Earth. Off to my left is a lake of brilliant blue water. It seems to be calling me. *Why not?* my inquisitive voice asks. *You might as well check this place out.* I must agree, because it is better than the dark lake with the wooden dock. I hope that I'll see Dad again;

after all, if it is my hallucination, then anything is possible, right?

As these thoughts appear in my mind, I am once more beside the lake.

I can get used to this moving from place to place without walking! Of course, I might never log in my daily ten thousand steps! My analytical, logical voice dampens my idyllic environment! I notice people walking down the beach holding hands, kids running about; the sounds of laughter drift over to me. My eyes spy a bench and just as suddenly a wave of tiredness sweeps over me. My exhaustion is at the point of me collapsing. Once more, just thinking about sitting on the bench instantly places me beside it. I flop down like a blob of goo; my muscles turn to gel. *So, this is how it is? You are a boneless sponge*, my analytical voice says.

"Cathy, sit up, don't slouch!" Mom's voice admonishes me. I slowly turn my head towards the voice while I attempt a better posture.

"Mom, what are you doing here?"

"Same thing I'm doing here!" Dad's voice replies from my other side. "We are together now, Cathy," Mom and Dad say together, "but it is not time for you to be here." Their expressions are stern, evoking no argument from me.

"Why?" I begin to cry. "I want to stay with you. I don't want to be alone."

"Honey, you will never be alone," Mom says; "we'll always be with you."

"Is Geoff here, too?" I ask, looking around for him.

"No, dear," Mom replies, "he went into the light. It was his time."

"We'll be here for you," Dad says, squeezing my arm.

"It's time," they say, standing up. Hand in hand, they walk away from me.

"Mom!" I shout. "Come back! Mom!"

***

Hands gently but firmly hold me down. "She's coming around. Ring for the nurse! Hell, ring for the doctor!" a husky voice shouts. A voice that somehow sounds familiar.

I open my eyes to look directly into Lou's face, which is hovering over mine. "Lou!" I cry. "What are you doing here?"

"What do you mean? You scared me half to death! I couldn't leave you all alone here. I sure as hell didn't want you to die all alone!" He chokes up, getting misty-eyed with his heartfelt words.

Then

Virgil held the wine to Geoff's glass and poured a little of the red liquid. Geoff lifted his glass, sniffed the wine's bouquet, then tasted it. He nodded his pleasure to the waiter, who proceeded to pour a generous amount of wine into each of our glasses. Satisfied, the waiter jammed the bottle into an ice bucket shaped like a wooden barrel, and left us to enjoy the wine.

"I believe that every soul has a partner, a soul mate," I said earnestly after my first sip of the Zinfandel.

"I feel so comfortable." He paused, taking a sip of his wine. "I feel so complete with you sitting here. I believe that you would understand anything I might tell you," Geoff said, taking my hand in his warm hand.

We sat, our hands entwined, resting on the table which looked like a very large wooden barrel. A wooden barrel that had its sides cut out to allow legs and feet to easily fit underneath. The top of the table had a gunnysack that was covered by a thick layer of clear plastic. In the middle of our table was a candle, its flame dancing in the breeze generated from the several large ceiling fans lazily circulating above our heads. The hushed sounds generated from the other people dining throughout the very large room floated over to us like a warm summer breeze. I felt as if we were completely invisible to the whole world. This was where I always wanted to remain. Fate, often envious of us mere mortals' happiness, had other plans in the making. Destiny was a bitch, but thankfully I was oblivious to what she had in store for us.

***

Each time Geoff kissed me, I felt weak in the knees. I had always thought this was just an expression, something authors wrote because it sounded so incredibly romantic. Geoff's kisses left no doubt to this misconception, as it happened to me each time he kissed me!

After several dates, we were once more outside of my door, trying to say goodnight. Tonight, our kissing could not satisfy the fire of desire burning increasingly hotter inside of each of us. Our lips remained hungrily seeking out the other, neither one of us wanting to let go. The urgency in our bodies wanted more satisfaction than hot, passionate kissing would bring. "Cathy...," Geoff started, unsure how to go about asking me.

"Yes," I breathed, answering his unasked question. I fumbled unlocking my door and opening it. Geoff and I almost fell into my living room.

Laughing, Geoff said, "I guess this makes it official, I am falling for you!" Geoff turned me around so I was facing him. He put his hands on the sides of my head, tilting my face up to his. His kiss, deeper, longer, and more demanding, set a firestorm of passion inside my body. My knees once more turned to jelly. Geoff picked me up in his strong arms, all the while kissing me more deeply than I had ever fantasized. I felt like I was floating.

Without conscious awareness, Geoff carried me to my bedroom and laid me gently on my hand-quilted red coverlet over my bed. Geoff positioned himself over me, his face inches from mine; his knees, holding his weight, were now on each side of my trembling body. His left hand began to gently stroke my breasts. Slowly, he began to unbutton my blouse. The eroticism of this unbuttoning ritual left me moaning in anticipation of what was to come.

I reached up to unbutton Geoff's shirt, but not with the same gentleness he had shown me. My desire to feel his bare, hairy, muscular chest against my bare skin was overpowering my sensibilities. Once his shirt was unbuttoned, we stopped with our attempts to undress each other. Each of us quickly finished removing our own shirts, then joined in another passionate, deep kiss. His hard body touching me aroused a primal sexual hunger deep inside my body – a part of my body that I never realized existed. *More! More!* my brain was screaming. "Please, more!" I moaned. I had never felt so hungry for intimate contact with another human being!

Geoff stopped kissing my breasts to pull down my jeans and panties.

I kicked them clear of my ankles. Geoff, too, had shucked his clothes and stood before me naked, his organ erect like a baton. When he bent over me, it was touching, stroking my pubic area. I felt warm and wet. Our bodies were ready, anxious for what was to come next. We continued to explore each other's body, kissing, stroking, touching, and teasing until we were ready to explode! "I'll try to be gentle," Geoff said huskily, "but I may not be able to control myself!"

"I don't care; rough or gentle, I just want you, now!" I moaned, unashamed of my animalistic desire for him.

Geoff entered me, gently at first. Moaning, I arched my back, encouraging Geoff to go deeper and deeper into me to satisfy my hunger for him. I moved my body closer to Geoff's, wanting to become one with him.

My fingers gripped his back in ecstasy while we kissed and came together in an explosion that left me sexually satiated and exhausted. Our cries and passionate groans came as one voice. Together, our cries ceased as we collapsed together. "Cathy, I love you!" Geoff huskily whispered.

"I love you, too!" I breathed, the words barely audible. My body was trembling from sexual ecstasy.

Geoff rolled over and turned towards me. We lay there staring at each other, feeling complete in our union. Geoff reached out with his hand and stroked my hair and then the side of my face. I could not expect to feel happier than this. "Will you move in with me?" Geoff asked.

"Isn't this too soon? We've just started going out?" I asked, although my mind was screaming, *yes, yes!* I had tears in my eyes, I was so happy.

"Cathy," whispered Geoff, "I have been longing for you for the past year! I should have asked you out sooner, but I thought you weren't interested in me. This isn't rushed for me, but if it is for you, I can wait, perhaps a week." Geoff gave a short, nervous chuckle.

Moments ago I thought I could not be happier, but I was wrong. Now I was happier than I had ever been in my entire life. For the first time I knew what it meant to feel like a woman. I loved this man more than life itself, and now I knew he loved me, too. I kissed him, holding him tight against my body. Geoff smiled at me in response and held me in his strong muscular arms. After a moment, when our breathing had been restored to normalcy, Geoff queried, "Does this mean that you'll move in with me?"

"No," I said, "but I will go with you to find our own apartment, our own place. A place we find together and where we can make our memories!"

Now

My eyes open when a hand pats my hand. "Good girl! You're back! Let me get the doctor!" The hand quickly leaves, and I notice that I am in a room shrouded in semidarkness. My eyes look about, taking in the bouquet of red roses.

"Geoff!" I croak.

"No," comes a husky, familiar voice.

"Lou?" I query. "Is that you?"

"Yeah," comes the gruff reply. "You've been in a coma for three weeks. We thought we were going to lose you, too."

"Geoff...," I start to say, but tears are already leaking from my eyes.

"He's gone, Cathy. I am so sorry."

"Why are you here? Where's my Mom?"

"Cathy," Lou clears his throat, then continues, "a lot has happened, but right now the doctor just wants you to rest."

"Ah, Ms Parker! I'm so happy to finally meet you!" says a pleasant voice from the doorway. Slowly, I turn my head to see a short, somewhat squat man in a white lab coat, so white it seems to be glowing in the dimly lit room. "My name is Dr Short. I am your neurosurgeon. You are doing very good, my dear. Now, let's see how the rest of you is holding up." His soft words soothe away my fears, my uncertainties, and ease my pain from the realization that Geoff is gone.

He takes my hands into his, hands so warm and so strong, just like Dad's. "Squeeze my left hand. Good. Now harder, please. Good, good. Let's try squeezing my right hand. A little harder. Excellent. Now close your eyes, Cathy." Fear streaks across my face. "Don't worry, Cathy. You are out of your coma." I physically relax, trusting this soft-spoken man. "Let's try that again without you looking at your hands." Fifteen minutes later, his preliminary exam is completed. "Ms Parker, you seem to have awoken with no serious complications; however, I will order a cranial CT scan for tomorrow morning to make sure there is nothing going on that shouldn't be."

"When can I go home?" I ask.

"Do you have someone to look after you?"

"Mom," I reply.

Dr Short's face is tinged with sadness. He turns to Lou. "Your mother suffered a stroke and died shortly after the, er, accident," explains Lou. "I am so sorry. Your brothers came and took care of everything, but they had to return to their jobs." Lou's voice trails off.

I am alone. I am an orphan. As these desolate words echo in my brain, I say, "I was talking to Mom, I am not sure when." Tears are flowing freely down my cheeks. Puzzlement creases my face.

"Cathy, your mother never got to come to your room." Emotion roughens Lou's gruff voice. Exhaustion floats into my being and my eyes slowly close to shut out the pain pressing down on my soul.

***

Beeping, rustling of clothes, carts carrying tubes for bodily fluids, and smells of food slowly rouse my consciousness. My eyes sluggishly open.

Streaks of daylight peek through the covered windows, illuminating the many colorful flowers. Bouquets of various sizes fill every space in my hospital room. Some flowers are bright and fresh, whereas others are beginning to droop and die. I slowly become aware of a deep, regular sound.

Realization dawns on me. Someone is snoring nearby! "Geoff?" I weakly ask.

I hear a grunt and then Lou's sad and haggard face appears over mine. "No, Cathy, it's me, Lou. Do you remember the police coming to my office to inform you that Geoff died?" he asks, his voice rough with emotion.

Sadness slaps into me, tears start to flow. "Geoff was killed," I sob. I am bombarded by these hurtful memories.

"Yes, but right now you must work on getting better. You've been hurt, bad. The doctors say it's a miracle you're alive!"

"Hurt?" I ask. Hurt how, I wonder; but I only say, "Is that why I hurt all over?"

"Yes. You can hit this button when you need more pain medicine."

"Thanks, Lou." I stifle a yawn. "But why am I so sleepy?" My voice seems to be coming from far away.

"Cathy, sleep is good. Sleep is how your body heals," Lou's softly spoken words carry me off to blissful oblivion.

Then

Our new apartment condo was located in a newly designed dark beige three-story building. The main floor was a fully equipped fitness center, open to residents at no extra cost, as well as to non-residents for a monthly fee. The upper two floors were made into geometrically unique condos.

Each apartment had a balcony that was either in the shape of a blue circle or a beige oval. It gave the impression that the building was winking at the rest of the city. Our new home was on the top floor, apartment 214. "Our new lucky number," Geoff said as we approached the door to our new home. At the door, Geoff stopped, turned to me and said, "Even though we aren't married, I want to carry you across the threshold – for luck!" Laughing, I gladly let him sweep me up in his arms and carry me into the apartment.

"Honey, you can carry me into our home today and every day for the next seventy years!" I said as I hugged him.

"Beautiful, I'm not sure about the next seventy years, but I will until my back won't allow it!" Geoff laughs.

The apartment looked different now with all the boxes left by the movers. It was no longer spacious but congested, like Saskatoon streets at rush hour. "I hope we have enough room!" I joked. We walked out onto our balcony in the shape of a blue circle and kissed.

"We may have to sleep out here if we don't get to unpacking!" chuckled Geoff as we stood, holding hands and looking out at the city.

Looking into his beautiful electric blue eyes that seemed to melt my whole body, I asked if he had a plan to the unpacking.

"Why, beautiful," he said, and my face blushed at his compliment, as I was still not used to someone calling me beautiful, "I am going to attack our bed. I hope that we will be able to go to bed early tonight!" His eyes twinkled mischievously. "You can put away the pots and pans and…"

***

We spent the next several months enjoying each other; sitting and talking, going for long walks, and turning our sexual fantasies into reality. One evening, after enjoying a barbecued supper of steak and baked potatoes, Geoff pushed back his chair. I turned my attention from looking at the city, the trees softly moving in the breeze, and asked, "What?"

"Cathy, I think we should think about getting married."

"Was that a proposal?" I asked jokingly.

"Not romantic enough for you?"

I just sat there with a look of incredulity on my face. Geoff smiled, turned and snapped open his briefcase which was propped against our balcony railing. When did he put his briefcase there? We always kept our briefcases in our office. Geoff pulled out a small blue velvet box. He held it out to me. I slowly reached for it. I inhaled deeply. I had dreamed of this moment for decades, and now that it was here I didn't want to rush it. "Actions speak louder than words," Geoff said, with emotion evident in his voice. I gingerly took the small box in my trembling fingers. "Open it!" Geoff urged me, as I continued to sit holding this small life-altering jewelry box.

I slowly opened its lid, exposing a large glittering red stone. "It's beautiful!" I exclaimed, feeling like a child on Christmas morning. Sitting on its own pedestal of pink velvet sat a ring. Two glittering diamonds sat flanking a large, dazzling red ruby. Tears were threatening to start tumbling down my cheeks. I didn't dare say anything.

"Well, do you like it?" asked Geoff, uncertainly.

"It's beautiful!" I exclaimed.

"So, your answer is 'yes'?"

"Yes!" I smiled and looked into Geoff's eyes. I was still incapable of speech.

"Do you know why I chose the ruby and two diamonds instead of the solitaire that I know you like?" Geoff asked.

"I don't know why you chose this, but I can tell you what it means to me," I offered. Confidence was back in control, confidence from my knowledge that we loved each other.

"Go ahead, tell me what it means to you, and who knows, I might just use your meaning!" Geoff chuckled.

"The ruby symbolizes July, when we found each other," I began. Geoff smiled, nodded and leant over to kiss me deeply. "The diamonds represent love eternal, our love for each other, for all times!" I looked at Geoff and was surprised to see his eyes were wet.

"Cathy, the ruby is as precious as our life over the past short year. We seem to know what the other is thinking even before we speak. You have said it better than I could ever have! I love you, Cathy: this moment" – Geoff took the ring out of the box – "tomorrow" – he set it on the tip of my finger – "and forever!" he finished, sliding the ring into place. The fit, like our love, was perfect!

***

The date was set: 31st July. This would give Geoff time to finish his current investigative assignment. We planned a small wedding, family and a few friends. We booked off three weeks from the newspaper for our honeymoon.

One night, while we were working on our respective laptop computers in our king-size bed, Geoff exclaimed, as he closed his laptop lid, "Cathy, this story is going to be the best story of my career! I know I have just scratched the tip of the iceberg. This is big, possibly the biggest crime story in the province! I will finish writing the first part of the story before our wedding, and then when we return from our honeymoon..." He paused, kissing me.

"To Cancún!" I added, pulling back to close my laptop so I could snuggle closer to him. I never wanted to be apart from him.

"I will write the second segment!" he finished confidently. "I have a little more investigating to do, which I plan to finish when I leave tomorrow. When I return, I will have everything I need to expose this criminal!"

"Maybe I could co-write with you on part two," I suggested, becoming a reporter once again.

"Robin" – Geoff said my pseudonym name I used in my reports – "that would be great; but I will have to ask my wife!" he finished, laughing.

"Seriously, what are you investigating? You've been working on this for a long time, and you haven't shared anything with me!" I pouted. "Aren't we supposed to be partners in life, in love and in work?"

"It's not that I don't want to share this story with you, but it could be very dangerous." Geoff's face turned very somber. *And maybe too close to home for you*, he thinks to himself.

"How long do you plan to be gone now?" I asked, as goose bumps rose on my arms. A feeling of dread spread over me, and I shivered.

"Hey, beautiful," Geoff said, folding me tighter into his arms. His warmth felt so good, but the feeling of bone-deep sadness stubbornly remained. "I should be home in a week. Then we can talk about Robin co-authoring on this piece!"

"Darling," I whispered, "you may work with Robin, but remember who loves you and who needs you right now!" I said with unabashed sexual need heavy in my voice. I playfully pushed Geoff over onto his back. I laid on top of Geoff and started to caress his chest with my fingers. Geoff responded by cupping my face in his strong hands and kissing me deeply. The rest of the night was lost to sensual fantasies that we made real. Much, much later, blissful sleep came to us. I had never felt so safe, so wanted and so loved in my entire life.

Geoff had gone to get the needed information for his explosive exposé, and I went to work each day. I worked diligently, finishing my seemingly unimportant stories, all the while dreaming of our three-week honeymoon booked in the honeymoon suite at the Sandos Cancún Luxury Resort. I was thankful these were small tasks, as my thoughts continuously returned to Geoff, our lovemaking, my happiness, and how I missed him even for a few days! My reverie was interrupted by my paper-covered intercom phone ringing.

Uncovering my desk phone, I picked up the telephone handset. "Cathy" – the metallic voice belonged to Lou Klassen, my editor – "would you come to my office?" Lou's voice sounded husky, as if he was suffering from a cold. *If he is catching a cold, I better not catch it and spoil my honeymoon*, I thought, smiling at the words 'my honeymoon'!

I briskly replied, "Right away, sir!" I hung up my phone and pushed back from my desk. I stood up, stretching the kinks out of my back. I straightened my suede leather skirt, thinking how Geoff loved its feel and how it aroused him whenever I wore it. I smiled at the different ways I was able to tease him, ending with our lovemaking! These thoughts warmed me, making my steps light. I walked out of my office and down the short hallway to Lou's office.

Lou's door, made of oak, had a light finish that shone in the dimmed lighting of the hallway. I paused outside of his door as a shiver of dread ran down my spine. I was hesitant to knock. In fact, I suddenly had the urge to lock myself in my office until Geoff returned. *Don't be silly!* my rational voice admonished. *Knock and act like the investigative reporter you want to be!* Bolstered by these words, I squared my shoulders and knocked.

Silence, then a soft, "Come in, Cathy." Lou's voice seemed husky, or perhaps tense was a more apt description. A coldness crept over my body; unexpectedly, my soul was filled with dread. *Lou wants an update on my stories*, I promised myself. I once more squared my shoulders, took a deep breath, then grabbed the doorknob and opened the door.

Lou's office, as usual, was encased in shadows. Most of the sunlight was kept outside by the partly closed heavy drapes. Lou got up from his massive brown leather chair that groaned in appreciation at the loss of Lou's excessive weight. Lou was a big man, often being mistaken for a retired fullback on the Saskatchewan Roughriders football team. Lou's size was intimidating until you got to know him. Once you knew the man, you discovered that he had a heart as soft as the jelly in his favorite coffee snack, bismarcks! As he came around his desk, he offered me a drink. "Lou, thanks, but it is too early to have a drink!" I laughed, as my body started to tremble uncontrollably.

"Sit down, Cathy." Lou steered me to a large tan-colored armchair. Lou's office was done completely in tones of brown. When I asked him why he chose shades of brown, he merely said it was to help him to not think about the evils of life. Brown symbolized the earth, pure and not hateful, always present, and never deceitful, a constant in his life when life was just the opposite. These thoughts came to me as I tried to quench the fear that had already gripped my soul. Settling into the armchair, I noticed for the first time a stranger sitting in the second chair in Lou's office. He was about fifty, his hair was mostly gray, and his skin was tanned and weathered. He looked at me with his soft brown eyes – so much like the deer from my fateful childhood hunting trip. His suit was the Sears bargain-basement type. I looked expectantly at Lou, then at the stranger. The silence was heavy, pressing down upon my chest. I found breathing difficult.

The stranger got up and walked over to me. "Ms Parker," he said, extending his hand, "my name is Detective McNeil." I limply shook the proffered hand, dropping my hand back onto my lap. He looked over to Lou, who nodded. He sat down beside me and said, in a well-rehearsed solemn voice, "I regret to inform you…" He paused, as if uncertain how to proceed. He cleared his throat, then continued, "Your fiancé, Geoff O'Connor, is dead. I'm sorry, Ms Parker, but it appears that he was killed very early this morning."

The floor swept up and wrapped its arms about me. I saw all the shades of brown in Lou's office starting to move about me in a swirl of browns. I was no longer aware of my body, Lou or Detective McNeil. A far-off sound, as if coming from a tunnel, grew in clarity until I heard my name being called. Who was calling me? Lou. Why is Lou calling me? Even my inner voices were at a loss. *Where am I?* I thought groggily to myself. *I think I'll just rest a bit.*

Strong hands were on my arms, and I felt myself being lifted, up, up, up. My body had lost its definitive shape as I was positioned in the armchair from which, moments ago, I had flowed out of like a slinky toy. Only now did I realize that I had fainted. Instantaneously, I remembered Detective McNeil's words. I forced myself to ask, "Geoff is dead, killed? But how, why, when?" Slowly, I brought my eyes to focus upon the men in the room. "Are you sure it's Geoff?" I asked, unable to believe his words.

"At this point we know it's Geoff O'Connor, but we do not know who killed him," said Detective McNeil. Lou stood looking down at the floor, not trusting his eyes to meet mine.

"You are?" My voice trailed off.

"Did you forget?" asked Lou, clearing his voice. "This is Detective McNeil from the RCMP."

I nodded. "Detective McNeil, what happened? You said killed! Who would want to kill Geoff?" I sobbed.

"At the moment we don't have all the answers. All we know is that he was found twenty kilometers east of the city. He was hit by a high-caliber bullet while driving his Ford Escape. It was probably fired from a rifle, perhaps a hunting rifle of unknown caliber. We don't expect to find the bullet as it went through his chest and exited through the side of his Ford Escape. We're looking for a spent casing, but we're not hopeful as the terrain is full of bush, sloughs, and wild prairie grass. In addition, we're not sure exactly where the rifle was fired from, because his body was moved and dumped in some bush that was growing a short distance from his abandoned vehicle. A farmer, who was looking for a lost calf, found him at five this morning. We estimated that he was killed some time earlier this morning, probably between one and three o'clock. He died instantly." The seasoned police detective looked uncomfortable. "Do you know of anyone who would have done this?"

I continued to sit and stare blankly at him, not wanting to believe him and hating him for telling me. My brain was refusing to comprehend his words.

"I'll take care of her," I heard Lou tell the detective.

"If you think of anyone who would want to hurt Geoff, please feel free to call me, any time, day or night." Detective O'Neil stood and extended his business card with his name and his contact numbers imprinted upon it. I stared at it, unmoving, uncomprehending. Lou came to my side and took the card.

"Thank you, Detective O'Neil," Lou said. "If Cathy thinks of anything, I'll let you know." I heard Lou's door open and close.

"Cathy, I am so, so very sorry!" Lou said, his voice cracking with emotion. "Geoff was such a good man! He didn't deserve to die! He had so much to live for!"

I broke down sobbing. My life was over.

Now

Sobs wrack my body, shaking me awake. Slowly, I become aware that I am lying in a hospital bed. I begin to open my eyes, but then shut them tight when my room starts to spin around and around. I feel like I am falling out of my bed. My hands grab for the bed's rails. I hang on as my stomach starts to heave.

Instantly, a cool cloth is placed on my forehead and a bodiless voice advises, "Just turn your head to the side if you feel like throwing up. We're here to help."

Slowly, the bed ceases to tip and the room ceases to spin. I open my eyes, ready to slam them shut again if the room begins to spin and tilt. I see a woman with long braided hair holding a cloth to my face.

"Thank you," I say softly. "Why am I feeling dizzy? Why do I feel like I am falling out of my bed?" I weakly smile and add, "Thanks for the rails!"

"Oh, honey, you have suffered a significant brain injury."

"A brain injury?" I ask, truly puzzled. "How?"

"For the time being we're going to let you heal and allow your memory to return on its own. We don't want to rush your progress. It is going to take time and lots of rest."

"And my other pains?" I prompt.

"You've suffered a broken arm, several broken and cracked ribs, and a dislocated knee. Those are healing nice. We have reduced your pain medicine to Tylenol Extra Strength. This shows just how quickly you are healing."

"Thank you," I mumble as my eyelids slowly close, and I drift back into darkness and peace where there is no pain. Where there is no grief.

Then

"He-hello," my breaking voice croaked haltingly into the cold, hard, plastic phone.

"Cathy, is that you?" inquired my mother's voice.

" Hmm," I said, not wanting to be talking on the phone, not wanting to be awake and not wanting to be living. Time had stopped for me since Geoff's death and his funeral.

"I want you to come and spend some time with me. I don't think it is good to be alone in that large apartment." Mom paused, waiting for a response. When nothing was forthcoming, she asked, "Cathy, Cathy, are you still there?"

"Yeah, Mom, I'm still here," my dull, lifeless voice responded.

"Well, will you come to Keysound? Spend some time to heal on the farm?" Mom's voice sounded concerned, which was not usual for her.

"All right, I guess for a few days," I said without enthusiasm. "I will drive out tonight."

I hung up, not waiting for a reply. I got up slowly from our bed and went to the bathroom. I was startled to see an old woman looking back at me in the mirror. Grief had its own way of sucking the essence of life out of a person.

"You are beautiful!" I could hear Geoff's voice telling me. "I will love you forever!"

Tears flowing like Niagara Falls, I sobbed, "Till death do us part!" I had never realized how ominous those words sounded until just now. "Geoff, you are going to always be with me." My sobs gradually lessened, and, with a quivering voice, I said, "I will not let your love be taken from me like your life. I will go on living, as meaningless and as hard as that might be. I know you would want me to. I will look after myself. I will be that beautiful woman you fell in love with!" For the first time since hearing about Geoff's death, I did feel slightly better.

After taking a steaming shower, the first since Geoff's funeral, I went into our office. Geoff and I each had our own desk and computer terminal. I sat in Geoff's chair. I could still sense his manly smell. How I yearned to hold him! Unexpectedly, a peacefulness covered me, like a soft velour blanket. My head gradually descended to rest upon Geoff's desk while I drifted off into oblivion.

A few hours later, a stabbing pain in my kinked neck rudely woke me from a dreamless sleep. Along with the gut-wrenching feeling of loss was a new feeling – a feeling of motivation. I now had a plan, a purpose. I was going to complete Geoff's final explosive exposé.

I touched the keyboard on his laptop, automatically booting up his Surface Pro. I scanned his files. Nothing noteworthy was discovered there. I was just about to shut his computer down when I decided to do a search of his ongoing story.

Geoff and I would hide files and then challenge each other to search for a hidden file. It was our version of 'hide and seek'. I decided to search for the keywords George_#1.

This was to be Geoff's best story ever. Geoff usually believed that each new story was going to be his best one ever!

Consequently, each story was numbered one until the next story came along!

He was so predictable! A faint smile appeared on my lips.

Geoff, like myself, wrote under a pseudonym; his was George Adams.

Geoff pretended to be a janitor at the *Wheatland Daily*, while I pretended to be an administrative assistant. We hid our real jobs from both of our families. My Mom didn't like Geoff, no matter how interesting he was to talk to, because he was a janitor! If only she knew the truth! I hit Enter. The search engine started searching for the file George_#1 in the 1TB of Geoff's storage on OneDrive. I went into the kitchen for a drink.

I heated a mug of coffee in the microwave oven, wondering when I had made this coffee. Does coffee spoil? As I waited, I saw the red light on my answer machine blinking. I pressed play. 'Cathy' – my mother's voice sounded edgy with worry – 'oh, I hate talking on these machines [a pause]. Anyway, you are not here, are you still there? [a longer pause] This is stupid! Of course you are not there! If you are out and return to your apartment, please phone me. I will phone if you're not here by ten. I hope everything is okay.' The machine clicked off just as the microwave shut off. I reached into the microwave, retrieved my steaming mug of questionable coffee and returned to my office. I planned to phone Mom when I finished my search.

Hmm, now it's 'your' office; how soon you forget! I smiled sadly as my mind mimicked Geoff's voice. "Oh, Geoff," I sobbed, "why did you leave me? I needed you." I was almost able to hear Geoff's voice questioning me about the wisdom of the goal I had set for myself. "Oh, right, Geoff, too dangerous for a girl!" I said to the empty apartment, and I smiled properly for the first time in days. The smile felt strange and unnatural on my face. It felt good!

Our office, like the rest of the apartment, was furnished with black leather and chrome furniture. The walls were painted a pale gray. The floors were hardwood in the kitchen, dining room, and office. The remaining floors in our two-bedroom apartment were carpeted in a thick-pile rug with shades of brown sprinkled throughout the tan base color. Geoff had chosen this rug, saying that whenever we walk on it, we would be able to pretend that we were walking on the beach! I walked back into our office and settled into Geoff's chair. A victorious smile spread across my face when George_#1 appeared on the monitor's screen.

"I haven't lost my touch!" I said triumphantly to the empty apartment. Smiling, I bent over to double click the file, and in less than a second the file opened. I straightened and sipped my heated coffee. At the top of the word document was a title, written in bold type. As my eyes read it, I gasped, my coffee cup slipping from my hands and spilling its contents on the hardwood floor. *Hey, Beautiful, if you are reading this, then I am dead.*

Tears began to surge in torrents out of my bloodshot eyes. Ragged cries of unintelligible anguish ripped out of my heart. "Oh, Geoff, why didn't you tell me? I could have helped!" I moaned to his computer.

Now

I feel like a vampire! Any amount of sunlight shining into my room sets up drills in my head, burrowing through my brain. The drapes are to be pinned closed. Only the dimmest night lights don't hurt my head. Curtains are also pulled around my bed to prevent hallway lights from coming in.

I hear my room's door open, then swish closed. "Lou?" I tentatively call out.

"Yes, it's me," comes the answer. "How'd you know? Do you have superpowers now?" He chuckles at his own joke. Drapes move and Lou appears beside my bed in my dusky cocoon.

"No, I just recognize your walk and your squeaky shoes!" It feels good to have a moment of normality.

"I brought you some word puzzles," Lou says as he hands me a stack of paperback puzzle books. "Dr Short said you should start working on these."

"Thanks, Lou," I say, uncertainly looking through the stack of books. Sudoku, word searches and crossword puzzles each in large-print format. Slowly, I am beginning to cope with large type for short periods of time. "How long should I spend on these?"

"Dr Short said to spend fifteen to thirty minutes at a time as many times a day as you can."

"What if I can't do these puzzles?" When I see Lou's panic, I add, "I was never much good at Sudoku or crossword puzzles. I would cheat and look at the answers to successfully solve them!" I smile and Lou relaxes.

"Is there anything I can get you, Cathy?" asks Lou, ready to change the topic.

Yeah, Geoff and my Mom, an angry, pissed-off voice sneers. I swallow, ignore it, and suggest, "A McDonald's Quarter Pounder with cheese and a chocolate sundae would be heavenly!"

Laughing, Lou assures me that tomorrow he'll bring that in for my supper!

"Don't forget to bring me a cup of coffee, extra-large not medium, and black!"

Then

I drove my five-year-old red Mustang convertible into our driveway early the next morning. The yard hadn't changed since I was thirteen years old. The trees were just as large and just as green. The lawn was showing signs of the late summer sun. I slowly drove up to our family farmhouse. My mother's blue Taurus was parked in the driveway. Beside it was parked a black Dodge Ram three-quarter-ton truck. I didn't recognize the vehicle. I parked behind Mom's car. The house beckoned me to come in, just as it had done almost thirty years ago!

I walked to the door and opened it. I heard my Mom talking to a man. Strange, I thought. My Dad had died years earlier and my Mom was running the farm herself. *Perhaps I should have come home more often*, I mused to myself. *Mom has been holding out on me!* A slow smile made its way onto my lips.

"Mom!" I called. "I'm home!"

"Cathy, you're here!" said Mom as she came into the entranceway. We hugged. "I thought you had changed your mind about coming! We have company. You knew him when he was younger," Mom was saying, her words tumbling over each other in her excitement to see me. "Horace; you remember, Cathy?" Mom asked. Then, lowering her voice, she turned to me, adding, "At least he didn't take after his father!"

"Cathy, my God you haven't changed!" Horace exclaimed, standing up as we walked into the kitchen. "I was so sorry to hear about Geoff." When he saw my puzzled look, he quickly added, "Your mother told me about his fatal car accident. City driving can be dangerous!"

"Oh, thank you," I stammered, remembering that the police and Lou felt it prudent to keep the facts of Geoff's death from the public. I was suddenly feeling very uncomfortable knowing that Geoff's killer was someone from my home area. Geoff's files were made up of notes done in shorthand with initials that only Geoff would understand. The only thing that was clear was that the epicenter was here, and I was here to find the truth!

"Cathy, would you like a cup of coffee?" asked Mom.

"Yes, thanks," I said. I joined Horace at the kitchen table while Mom poured my cup of coffee.

"So, Cathy," started Horace, "are you going to be around for a while?"

"Yeah, I am planning on staying for a month or so," I said. Mom set the full cup of coffee in front of me and joined us at the table, along with a plate of chocolate chip cookies, my favorite since I could eat solid food!

"Oh, Cathy, that is wonderful!" Mom successfully hid her surprise with this announcement.

"That will be nice for your Mom," Horace agreed. He sipped his coffee looking at me, studying me. His blue gray eyes seemed to be scanning me, seeking out my secrets.

I smiled and busied myself with taking a sip of coffee and reaching for a cookie. I looked at him over my steaming cup of coffee. He looked like he did so very long ago, only with more lines, which gave him a worldly persona. I felt warm and safe and, yes, like a young girl free of all life's pain.

I pulled my eyes away and looked at Mom. "I have to go outside and bring in my suitcases." Feelings were being resurrected inside of my heart, feelings that belonged to a teenage girl long ago. Feelings that seemed to betray Geoff.

"Let me help," offered Horace as he quickly got up and followed me outside.

I walked in front of Horace, remembering the last time we came out of our house together, that day almost thirty years ago. I could still hear the rain in my mind. Horace was going to show us the slide in the loft. He was cute; no, handsome. I was in love with him then, but now? Could I be falling under his spell? *No, you idiot! You're ready for anything because of your loss. You just want the peace of your childhood to return and heal you*, my analytical brain scolded me. Suddenly, I shuddered, feeling my eyes becoming wet. *Oh, Geoff, I miss you so much!*

"Cathy," Horace's voice broke through my thoughts, "can you pop open the trunk?" He was standing by the trunk, pointing at the remote keyless entry keyfob, which I held in my hand. "Do you remember the first time I saw you?" he asked, as if he was reading my thoughts.

"Yeah, I remember," I said as I obligingly hit the blue button with a picture of an open trunk. The trunk's latch clicked open. Horace lifted the lid, exposing my two suitcases. My face felt hot with the memories of my desires.

"I know you are not ready to date," Horace started, paused, and then quickly finished, "but do you think two childhood friends could go out for a beer or something?"

"That would be nice," I replied. I felt that to relive some teenage fantasies would be a much-needed break from the grief I felt as a woman who was in love and who, if I were to be honest with myself, was still in love. This would also prove helpful to produce the information I needed to continue the investigation that Geoff started and was killed over. Horace would be an ideal person as he knew everyone in the area. "I haven't talked about my childhood for a long time! I think that is just what the doctor ordered, to relive some pleasant memories with a friend! When?"

Horace's face lit up, making me feel guilty as his feelings seemed to be more intense, feelings that were more than just of a friend. "Well, maybe tomorrow night. It will give you time to settle in."

"Great, tomorrow night at about eight o'clock," I said, smiling and thinking that I was just using him for information, but I was also going to be sharing memories with him.

"See you at eight," said Horace as he picked up my two suitcases. I reached into my car and took out my Apple PowerBook. Together, we walked back into the house. My body was tingling for the first time in a long while. Was this a betrayal of Geoff's memory? No, it was just a memory of a young girl's fantasy, nothing more. This was my first step to reconstruct Geoff's last week of life. This was my first step to find Geoff's killer.

As the time of my date with Horace grew nearer, I became increasingly tense. I was not pleased with anything I saw reflected in the mirror which was attached to my dresser. *What is wrong with you? It is only Horace!* my critical inner self started to scold me. *How can you think of another man when it has been only a month since Geoff's death?* my heart sobbed. *This is for Geoff!* I silently shouted in my mind, silencing any further debate about the wisdom of my actions. Besides, sharing stories with a childhood friend will be relaxing and it will give me a chance to meet more people in the area. Yes, it will feel good to remember that long-ago teenage girl and her fantasies. I decided to pull on a pair of old blue jeans and a light blue summer pullover sweater.

Oooh, a sweater, so much the nicer to run his hands over you! my dreamy voice cooed. *Quiet!* I smiled at my youthful fantasy of Horace's hands on my breasts, on my legs, holding me tight. I took one last look in the mirror and accepted the way I looked. I turned around and shut off the light. I walked down the hallway into the kitchen.

Mom looked up from the newspaper she was reading and said, "Cathy, you look terrific!"

"Thanks, Mom," I said, settling myself onto a chair by the wooden kitchen table. "What are you reading?" I asked, wanting to change the subject.

"Oh, I am reading this article about teens stealing GM cars and taking them for joy rides in Saskatoon. I am also reading it because it is written by my favorite writer, Robin McCathy!"

My head jerked up at the mention of my pseudonym. "What did you say, Mom?" I asked, trying to cover the fact that she was talking about me!

"Robin, my favorite writer at the *Wheatland Daily* paper! Do you know Robin? Is Robin a woman or a man? What is she or he like?"

"Whoa, Mom!" I said, laughing. "I am Lou's administrative assistant, a secretary at the paper. I don't know Robin, but then I don't know many of the reporters at the paper."

"Too bad," Mom sighed. "Don't get me wrong, Geoff was a nice person, even if he was only a janitor. To be honest, I always thought you could have done better."

Anger flared inside of me, but before I could fire a deadly shot back, the doorbell rang. Horace had arrived. I got up and hurried to the back door to greet him.

Horace was standing outside the door, looking like he did so very long ago. He still had that casual way about him. He was even sexier than I remembered when we were kids! My breath caught in my throat. I felt thirteen again!

Horace opened the door wide for me to come out. "Wow, Cathy, you look like a million bucks!" Horace said, a big lopsided grin affixed to his sensual lips.

"Thanks, you look pretty great yourself," I said as I took in his Western blue plaid shirt that was tucked into his form-fitting blue jeans.

"Enjoy yourself, Cathy. I will leave the light on for you," Mom called out as I stepped through the open door into the evening dusk characteristic of the country. No light pollution interfered with a person's enjoyment of twilight in the country.

"Where are we going?" I asked, suddenly feeling unsure about my feelings and myself. *Are you really ready for this?* my heart wisely asked.

Horace took my hand and guided me to his freshly washed black truck, held open the door and helped me inside. Momentarily confused, I thought it was Geoff. I stopped myself from saying Geoff's name when I stuttered, "Th-thank y-you." I settled myself by the door and did up my seatbelt. Horace got in the other side and did up his seatbelt. Silence hung inside the truck cab. A feeling of unease started to creep over me. Was it too soon to indulge in my childhood fantasies? Would I remain in control? Would I seek information like a good investigative reporter, or would I just try to live out my childhood fantasy with this man, this stranger? Horace was no longer a boy but a man, a very sensual man.

As we pulled out of the yard, Horace said, "Cathy, come closer. I don't bite unless you want me to!" The request was accompanied by his usual sensual smile. My heart fluttered with my still-remembered teen crush! I undid my seatbelt and slid over to sit beside Horace. Instantly, his arm rested on my shoulder as his hand moved to my face to begin stroking my right cheek. Bolts of electricity shot off inside of me. "Do you like that?" Horace asked boldly.

"Uh," I stammered, "yes, in fact I do," I said haltingly.

"Do you want me to stop?" he asked, his voice full of want. "I don't want to rush you," he said, his voice tender and hushed.

"No, don't stop." I paused, and then, sadness evident in my voice, I continued, "I loved Geoff and I miss him so very much."

"A woman like you, once you've known real love, needs to be loved. It is criminal to have someone like you left behind to wither up and die!" Horace said, compassion strong in his voice.

We drove silently, Horace purposefully taking left turns more aggressively than necessary so I would slide closer. It also allowed his hand to dip lower and closer to my breast. I smiled at this boyish attempt to touch my breast. I felt flattered and lonely and sensual and needy. We continued winding through country dirt roads until the lights of Keysound twinkled on the darkened horizon. Minutes later, Horace pulled his Dodge Ram in front of the town's only bar. Horace got out of the truck and hurried around to hold open my door.

"Here we are!" Horace said pleasantly. He took my hand and led me into the noisy bar. A jukebox was playing 'Oh, Lonesome Me' by the Kentucky Headhunters. Two couples were dancing on the small dance floor, bumping and grinding to the rhythmic beat blasting through the bar's speakers. Most of the tables were in use by groups of people drinking, laughing, and talking. Horace steered me over to a table off to the side.

"Hi, Horace!" said a grizzled man; gray sprinkled his dark hair. "Who in hell is this pretty little filly?" he asked, slightly slurring his words.

"Hey, Tyrell, this here is Cathy Parker," Horace answered with a smile that started and ended on his lips. His eyes were surprisingly emotionless.

"Cathy Parker," the older man said. "Are you any relation to, ahh, Frank Parker?"

"Frank was my Dad," I said, eager to be free of this man who Horace certainly did not like.

"Frank was a damn fine man," he said, lifting his beer to his lips and taking a long drink from it. "Why in hell would you want to be out with a Moonie? Good God, girl, I could tell you some stories about these here Moonies!"

I felt Horace stiffen as anger started to radiate from him. The reporter inside of me came awake, wondering what, if anything, this very thin old man could tell me about the suspected hit man in this area. Could it be that his information might point me at the man who killed Geoff? I made a mental note to talk to him later.

"Talk to you later," said Horace. Did I detect a threat in his voice? Tyrell didn't seem threatened. Horace guided me over to the lone empty table. "You must overlook Tyrell. I don't know if Frank ever spoke of him, but he was and still is the town drunk. He is harmless, but he doesn't care what he says. One day it could be his undoing." This time I was not mistaken. Horace's voice had taken on a steel, cold edge.

"Horace, don't let him upset you! Some old drunk is not going to spoil my evening with you," I said, while my reporter voice was jubilantly saying that he was just the man I must talk to! It wouldn't surprise me if Tyrell might have seen or heard something. So often the town drunk, the homeless person on the street, the elderly woman in her garden, is overlooked during an investigation when indeed this very person just might be the missing witness who could help solve a crime.

Horace stared deep into my eyes, his anger dissipating. My face flushed with the duplicity of my intentions! Horace's voice had softened, returning to that sensual voice that had captured my heart the first time we met. "Cathy, what would you like to drink?"

"A Harvey Wallbanger, please," I said with a slight unsteadiness in my voice. Was I imagining Horace's reaction to Tyrell?

Horace signaled for the barmaid to come over. An overweight woman who appeared to be in her early fifties came to our table. Her dyed blonde hair looked like a cumulus cloud balancing atop her head. Her black roots, like a thunderhead, fastened her hair to her scalp. Once you pulled your gaze from her hair, you took in the rest of this wannabe teenager. Her well-endowed chest was barely contained in a form-fitting, very low-cut T-shirt!

Across her breasts read, 'TIP me or DIE of Thirst!' Her ample hips were poured into a tight black miniskirt. Her sausage-like legs were squeezed into black fishnet tights. Living proof of just how strong nylon is! The outfit on her was like cold water being splashed on me! Sex was suddenly purged from my thoughts. "Hi, sexy," beamed the barmaid at Horace, bending down real low so he could get a better view of her voluptuous breasts, "what can I do you for?" The implication was so evident that I blushed in embarrassment at her boldness.

Horace acted the part of a most flattered man, saying, "Darling, a Harvey Wallbanger for my friend here and a beer on tap for me." His words were sensually spoken. The underdressed, overweight barmaid smiled and went for the drinks.

"Would you care to dance?" Horace asked.

"Yes," I replied, unsure what was expected. "I can't do the Texas Twostep!" I laughed nervously.

"Darling," Horace said, "I know just the right songs for you and me!" Horace quickly got up and strolled over to the jukebox. He seemed to know what effect those snug blue jeans were having on me, much less the barmaid. He leaned over the lighted window, studying the CDs. I realized that he had done this same performance many, many times. I smiled at how some men strut their stuff while Geoff just acted natural to melt my heart. However, his well-executed act once again ignited my sensual interest which moments ago had been doused. These physical sensations were troublesome. Guilt invaded me. I defended my unwanted feelings, rationalizing that I was just living out a fantasy that had laid dormant so long in my heart.

As Horace returned to the table holding out his hand, 'Stand By Me' by Ben E. King started to play on the jukebox. How did Horace know that this was my favorite song of my childhood? We danced slowly on the dance floor, at first tentative and unsure, but by the time the song ended we were dancing up close. 'Smoke Gets In Your Eyes' by The Platters started next, although I was hardly aware of a different song. Horace's breath was warm on my neck and his hands were exploring my back and squeezing my buttocks. My breath was raspy, my body warm and beginning to ache with desire of once again intimately knowing a man. "Horace," I hoarsely whispered.

"What, my love?" he asked in a low, husky whisper.

"I think we had better slow down! Let's have our drinks!" I suggested, pulling away from his increasingly aggressive touching.

Horace looked down at my face, kissed me lightly on the lips and led me back to the table. We sat and sipped our drinks while looking at each other and trying to make small talk. *You are out of control!* my ever-cautious conscience warned. I countered that I wanted to be alone with him to get information. What harm would there be to live out a girl's unfulfilled fantasy? I was in control of the situation. *You're deluding yourself,* stated my rational conscience.

"Cathy, let's get out of here!" Horace's voice interrupted my conflicting thoughts.

"Okay, let's go," I said, leaving my drink half full.

We walked out of the bar, hand in hand, and straight to his truck.

Horace opened my door and helped me climb inside. I buckled up by the door, not daring to come closer. Horace got in, shut the door, and started the engine. It roared to life. Horace jammed it into reverse and backed the truck out away from the curb. He smoothly slid the gearshift into drive and sped out of town. Within seconds we were speeding down country roads.

"Where are we going in such a hurry?" I asked, hiding my increasing concern as I was disorientated by the darkness.

"To my place," Horace said huskily.

"Are your parents still living on the farm?" I asked, not wanting to meet up with Floyd Moonie.

"Nah, my mother moved into town after my father died," Horace said, his voice lacking emotion.

"I'm sorry to hear about your dad," I softly said. Horace either didn't hear me or chose not to answer. Perhaps he wasn't sorry and didn't want to share that with me. I couldn't blame him!

We drove the rest of the way in silence. I had to think about what might happen. How far was I willing to go to gather information? Was I ready for this? Was it fair to Horace if my feelings were based on a teenage fantasy? My reluctance was also due to my omnipresent grief over Geoff.

Indecision continued to plague my mind as we crossed the Texas gate entering Horace's yard. It hadn't changed in all these years. He pulled the truck up to the front door. I could hear gravel crunching and feel the truck skid on the loose gravel as he braked sharply.

Wordlessly, Horace opened his door. He seemed to have been lost in thought just like I was. I felt certain his thoughts were not as muddled as mine. Quickly, he came around the cab, opened my door and held out his hand for me to take. I reached out and took his hand. The shot of electricity that passed between us shorted out any doubts about not going in. *Girl, you need to be loved by a man to be made to feel alive again.* My romantic heart was always up for a new love. *Go for it, girl!* Where was my logical voice? I could not think of any argument against going inside.

We entered the house and as we walked from room to room, Horace was turning on the lights. I found myself being led into a modestly furnished living room. The sparse furniture reflected Horace's lack of care for material things. Horace dropped my hand and switched on his satellite radio to a station that played rock'n'roll from the fifties and sixties. He stood there for a moment, staring straight ahead at the Walmart special entertainment center. I was about to ask what he was thinking, when he turned around to face me.

Horace had his shirt unbuttoned, exposing his hairless chest. I was drawn to him as if I was a puppet and he pulled my strings. His arms encircled me, pulling me closer to his body, which felt hot, firm, and sensual. I could feel the hardness between his legs and the wetness between mine.

We danced, or rather we moved sensually. Each of us had a common goal, to feel as much of the other's body as it was possible while fully dressed.

Horace's hand started to adeptly remedy this. I heard the zipper on my jeans being pulled down. I couldn't move away. An invisible force moved and pushed me even closer into his body. I barely noticed his hands searching inside my panties, touching me, arousing me. Involuntarily, I heard myself moan softly.

"Oh, Cathy," Horace said hoarsely, "I want you to take your sweater off for me." His hands were moving over my breasts, caressing them, gently pinching them. This was arousing me in such a way I never believed possible with so little skin being touched.

I looked up into his gunmetal blue eyes and shuddered. Why did I think gunmetal, violence, Geoff being gunned down in cold blood and soul-wrenching grief? I pushed away from Horace as my forgotten unzipped jeans hung open on my hips.

"Cathy," Horace croaked, "please. I really need you. I want you and I think you want me, too."

Tears were making my eyes glisten. I stood like a statue in the middle of the living room.

Horace tentatively lifted his hand to gently caress my face, my skin igniting under his touch. I shuddered. "Horace, I…," I croaked.

"Cathy, if I am just to be used to assuage your grief, I understand; but…" Horace pulled me closer, kissing, tasting my tears dripping from my eyes. "I have wanted you for years." I could hear his strong heart beating under his shirt. His warmth began melting my uncertainty, dulling my grief.

"Horace, it's just that I loved, love Geoff. I don't know what exactly I feel for you. I remember my childhood crush on you, but we're not kids anymore!"

"We also don't know what tomorrow will bring, either. You should know that better than anyone!" Horace started stroking my back, cupping my ass, his intentions still very evident.

Come on, Cathy, that insidious romantic voice urged, *you have dreamt of this moment ever since you were thirteen! Geoff won't mind, he'd want you to live, to feel alive. Don't forget the value of pillow talk; you might get some valuable information.* Now isn't that a kick in the pants? My starry-eyed voice was beginning to sound like my analytical self! *I'll take one for the team,* and I smiled.

Horace, seeing me smile, took my hand and began to urge me slowly toward the short hallway and his bedroom.

My legs, seemingly with a mind of their own, began to move down the narrow hallway.

At the end of the dimly lit hallway, we entered a large masculine-looking bedroom. Along the wall across from the door was a king-sized bed. A dark brown duvet covered its surface. Horace grabbed it and in one motion had it and the blankets underneath pulled back, revealing black sheets. "Were you expecting me, or do you always make your bed in the morning?"

Laughing, Horace said huskily, "I always make it each morning because you never know how the day will end!" He touched my sweater and asked, "May I help you with that?"

I stepped closer to him, raised my hands, and answered in a voice revealing my own sexual need, "Please."

Horace began to gently tug my sweater up, planting soft kisses on my stomach and working up. Each kiss had me trembling. *How can such a simple action become such a turn on?*, my analytical voice queried. "Hmmm," I answered.

Horace's eyes were once more unnervingly staring at me standing in my black lacy bra and unzipped jeans. "Like what you see?" I tried for sexy, but I felt that I failed.

"God, Cathy," Horace moaned, "I can't believe it. I have waited so long! God, what an idiot I've been!"

Looking at Horace and feeling somewhat lacking in the emotional exchange, I decided to become the woman I was when I was with Geoff. "I see only two things interfering with me getting to feel you against my naked body." I paused, looking into his eyes. Smiling, I unhooked my bra and shrugged it off, letting it land on the floor. "Now..." – again I paused, smiling – "I must do something else; I hope you won't mind!" Horace started to say something, when I slowly started to move my hands up from the tops of his jeans to the center of his chest, where I paused. Quickly, I grabbed his shirt's pearl snap closures and gave it one no-nonsense tug. Startled, Horace looked down at me and began to smile that wickedly, sexy smile that he had had since the first day we met.

"Why, honey, you missed one snap!" In one lightning-quick motion, he had his jeans off and had pulled me into his arms. Purposefully, we toppled onto his bed, laughing like two kids.

Horace grabbed the tops of my jeans and pushed them down over my feet. His mouth found mine and our tongues began to explore and taste each other. Coming up for air, Horace continued kissing me down my neck, my breasts, my stomach. I was quivering when Horace returned to my mouth.

I saw his muscled stomach, his organ swollen and hard and inviting. *God*, my romantic heart moaned, *he's so big!* Horace laid down on me, his elbows flanking me, and he took my nipples, one at a time, to suckle. His tongue was arousing me to an even higher level, a level I didn't think possible. I was lightheaded and breathless. Suddenly, Horace bit down. The pain was exquisite and erotic. I began moaning and moving under him, trying to get him to enter me and relieve this pressure that was sure to tear me apart. Still he played his tongue over my breasts. I was delirious with ecstasy. "Please, Horace, no more, I can't take it; please, please come inside of me now!" I begged hoarsely, moaning uncontrollably. I was withering under his body, pressing my body closer and closer to his to find release. My attempts only succeeded in arousing myself more.

"Cathy, I have wanted you from the first time I met you! Did you feel the same?" Horace was breathing heavily.

Quickly, Horace rolled off me and grabbed for the night table beside his bed. "One moment, darling," he said as he sheathed himself.

I idly wondered if it was possible to die while making orgasmic love. *Well, that would certainly be a great way to go!*, purred my heart. I could hear my logical voice laughing at the lunacy of these thoughts.

Our orgasmic lovemaking ended when Horace collapsed upon me. We were both breathing hard. He rolled off me, positioning himself to lie beside me, our sweaty, naked bodies touching as natural as the wind blowing in the trees. I had never known lovemaking to be so primitively intense!

"Cathy," Horace said a few minutes later, his hand caressing my face, "I love you and I have always loved you. When I heard of your engagement, I knew that I had made the worst mistake of my life. I should have come after you years ago, but I thought I had time, you know? Maybe it is too soon, but do you think that I might be able to make you happy, as happy as you have made me?" He quit touching me, choosing to turn to look directly into my eyes.

His blue gray eyes were bluer with his want, his need. "Horace, I loved Geoff, and no one will ever replace him; but I had loved you when we first met as kids! I thought you didn't feel the same way when we grew up!" I said with an honesty that I hadn't expected to share tonight or ever with Horace.

"What would give you that idea?" Horace asked. His confusion was clear in his expression.

"Horace, you practically ran from me after my Dad's funeral!" I said lightly.

"Ah, yes." Horace looked very uncomfortable. "Sorry. I didn't want to interfere with your education. I knew, from what your Dad shared, that your education was very important to you."

Trying to lighten the sudden seriousness, I quipped, "Why, Horace, I thought you were afraid of me becoming an RCMP officer!" I started to laugh, expecting Horace to join me, but my laughter died in my throat when I saw the coldness in Horace's eyes. "Hey, I can't fine you for speeding tonight, because I dropped out!"

I saw Horace forcibly neutralize the coldness in his eyes and he tried to add lightly, "I totally forgot that! Had I remembered you were attending the RCMP academy in Regina, I would not have been driving while distracted! In fact, I would have insisted you remain on your side of the seat with your seatbelt done up!" He chuckled, and his eyes were once again twinkling with mischief.

I smiled, but I couldn't help wondering what he was hiding. Our scorching passion of a few minutes ago had been replaced by a tingling sensation that Horace was hiding something that he was not willing to share even after our intense lovemaking.

"Cathy, will you stay here with me?" Horace seemed unaware of my cooled emotions, of my suspicions.

"No, I can't, not now," I said, remembering Geoff and remembering my purpose of being back home. I was uneasy spending the night with Horace. The earlier comfort I felt with him had been replaced with feelings of nervousness. My next words were chosen carefully. "Horace, I don't want an affair. I am still mourning Geoff. You were my first love, even if it only was a fantasy on my part!"

"This isn't going to be an affair; I want you with me," said Horace, his voice sounding rough with emotion. My silence prompted him to add, in a softer voice, "I want you to be my wife, sweetheart. I have always wanted you to be my wife!" he said, love evident in his voice.

"I had felt the same way when I was younger." I was beginning to feel cornered. "I don't want to use you for my own satisfaction." Horace smiled a wicked, sensual smile and kissed me long and hard. "I want to be sure of my feelings for you now, today, not from thirty years ago!" I said softly, hoping that he wouldn't misunderstand my wish to proceed much slower. When Horace didn't say anything, I asked, "Does this disappoint you?"

"Yes and no. I have waited for so many years, I guess I can wait a little longer!" He laughed and kissed me gently, holding me close.

I fell asleep in the arms of my first love. Sleep did not keep my brain from mulling over his reaction to what I had planned to be a lighthearted statement. Did he have a reason to fear the RCMP, or was it from growing up with Floyd?

Now

Lying back in my hospital bed, I feel exhausted. I shake my head in frustration at my ongoing weakness. Two hours working on puzzles, things I used to do for relaxation, leave me as tired as if I had put in a long day at work getting my copy ready to be submitted. "Man, I am a wuss!" I say cynically to my cocooned room. My curtains surrounding my dimly lit bed stir gently in the ever-present breeze from the air exchange.

"Nope, not a wuss, but someone on withdrawal from fast food!" comes a jovial voice.

"Lou? I must be dead, and this is heaven, because you never sound that happy!" I laugh as Lou's big frame emerges from between my curtains. Light shoots across my face, lacerating my brain. Agony squeezes my eyes shut. I involuntarily moan.

"Sorry, honey, I forgot!" Lou says, quickly drawing the curtains together. "Forgive me?" he asks, holding out the McDonald's bag and an extra large cup of McCafé – noir, of course.

How can I possibly stay mad at a man like that? "It's all right, Lou," I say, still wincing with the sharp pain cutting through my brain. "I must get used to daylight! I refuse to become a vampire – I hate my steak rare!" We both laugh. The tension of seconds before is forgotten.

"I checked with your doctor and he said that you can have your pain meds any time you want," Lou adds while he pulls out my Quarter Pounder with cheese, extra mustard and pickles. He sets the chocolate sundae next to the wrapped hamburger. He steps back as if to give me room to eat, reclaiming his personal chair. This chair was brought down from the doctors' lounge so Lou might sleep in it during his nightly vigils. Now it remains for his use during our daily visits. I smile, picturing Lou's large body utilizing the small plastic hospital chairs.

I grab the hamburger and rip off the wrapper, sinking my teeth into the warm meat and bun. "Oh God, this is so good!" I moan in ecstasy. "This is better than painkillers! Thank you, Lou!" I say with my mouth full. I know that I must look like I have been starved during my stay in the hospital, but right now I do not care!

"I didn't realize starving patients was part of the province's cutbacks in medical care!" laughs Lou.

"I heard that!" comes an indignant voice, followed by a stout, middle-aged nurse. Her long, dark hair is swept up into a bun on the top of her head. "I'll have you know I eat the same food as we feed the patients in the cafeteria, and I" – here she holds both hands out at her sides – "am far from being starved!" We laugh and once more I feel normal, whatever my new normal is!

"Dearie, do you remember my name?" She shoots Lou a look that silences his answering her question.

"Ah." My face shows the tension that always appears when I am struggling with my brain. "Lacy? Lana? No, that is not quite right, but I'm close, right?"

"You're getting there. Do you want me to tell you?"

Tears sting my eyes. "Yes, I just can't quite remember, again!"

"It's Lucy," she supplies.

"*I Love Lucy!*" adds Lou, then stops, mortified at what he just said. "I mean, if you remember something associated with a word then you can think your way to the answer! Do you remember the rerun of the *I Love Lucy* series on Netflix?"

"Yes, I love that series, as corny as it is!" I exclaim. "I will not forget your name any more!" I chuckle, my face glowing with newfound confidence.

Smiling, she busies herself checking my charts, my eyes – really shining a bright light into the eyes of a light-sensitive person, how cruel! "You know, dear, you are indeed eating my favorite McDonald's meal, minus the fries! I don't know how you can skip those!"

Chuckling, I offer, "The fries smell so good, too bad they don't taste as good as they smell!"

"How did the puzzles go today? I noticed you were diligently working on them this afternoon."

My face turns red with embarrassment as I reply softly, "I am not as proficient as I used to be. Sudoku, however, is about the same for me."

"You have just started, so don't be too hard on yourself," the nurse says, patting my hand like a mother encouraging her preschool child to continue practicing printing her name. "You will notice an improvement over time. You are doing very well. Well, I must see my other patients before I leave for the night. Do you need anything right now?"

"No, thanks," I say. "I've got everything I need!" My eyes suddenly well up with tears.

"See you tomorrow," the nurse offers. She turns to Lou to add, "And nice seeing you again, Lou." I notice Lou's face flush. Could it be my boss is interested in my nurse? I have never known Lou to date since I have been at the paper. I know he has been a widower for many years. I smile at my thoughts.

"What are you smiling at?" asks Lou in his usual brusque voice.

"Oh, just recalling the *I Love Lucy* episodes!" I lie smoothly.

Maybe I am indeed becoming my normal self.

Then

Horace lay watching Cathy sleeping. He gently ran his fingers through her long, thick, dark hair. Cathy moaned in pleasure, a small smile curving up her lips. He thought, *Can I have her? Can I be that lucky?* He softly pushed back a strand of hair that had toppled down over her eyes, threatening to tickle her nose. Horace bent over and softly kissed her soft, sensual lips.

He loved her long, soft, dark brown hair, her soft skin, her sweet chocolate brown eyes, her smell, and her sense of humor. In fact, if he was honest with himself – he smiled wryly at this notion of being honest – he had fallen hard for this girl that first morning his drunkard old man dragged him to visit the new neighbors! *Well, how about that*, he mused, *that old bastard has done one unselfish nice thing for me!*

Horace, feeling his arousal was about to start touching and teasing Cathy, chuckled softly to himself. "Nothing like a break-of-dawn encore performance!" His cell phone, like a jealous lover, started buzzing like a mad hornet in his jeans' pocket. "Shit!" Horace cursed softly. Carefully, he got out of bed and grabbed his discarded jeans lying in a pile beside the bed. No way was he putting the light on. *If I miss the call, then fun time for Cathy and me!* Picturing exotic activities this would entail, he quickly slipped into his jeans – commando, of course – and softly closed the bedroom door.

A hoarse, "Yes," was softly spoken into his iPhone as he walked barefoot down the hallway.

"Who's this?" a cautious voice asked.

"Who the fuck do you want to talk to?" growled Horace, his voice instantly becoming hard as granite.

"I, er, am answering your advertisement in the *Hunter's Guide*," stammered a tentative faceless voice. "I need your services for an... er, I need a hunting guide. I was told you're good." The voice trailed off, unsure how to proceed.

So much for a new life, he wearily thought with a heavy heart. "What do you want hunted?" he asked in a voice that was cold as glacier ice.

Silence on the phone. "Look," he growled, "if you don't know what you want, then fuck off! I'm busy."

Before he was able to disconnect, a panicky voice yelled out, "No, wait! I need you! A doe and a fawn!"

"I only hunt bucks," he coldly replied, each word aimed at this unseen caller like a fist to a boxing bag. His voice more like the growl of a wolf added, "And I'm retiring!" Horace hadn't intended to voice this but now that the thought was out he felt good. Could it be possible? His musings were ripped apart with a voice shouting out a long ago promise.

"Carlos said you owed him!" These words that he had hoped to never hear turned him into ice. Carlos had saved him from rotting forever in a backwoods jail in the Deep South. He knew he owed Carlos.

That night in Louisiana seemed so long ago. Carlos had invited him to join him on a fishing trip. Not just any fishing trip, but deep-sea fishing! How could he say no? He needed some R & R after their hunting trip.

Carlos had fucked up the whole hunting trip; the collateral damage that was avoidable with better preparation marked the end of their future hunting trips. Carlos, ashamed of his fuck-up, but, more importantly, his desire to not become collateral damage in the future, made an offer Horace could not say no to. A week of deep-sea fishing off Dauphin Island, Louisiana! To sweeten the pot, Carlos' car rental agency, 'CARs 4 U' in Mobile, delivered a red Dodge Viper SRT10 – an upgrade – to the airport in Mobile! Horace accepted Carlos' apology; but he was done hunting with Carlos. However, deep-sea fishing – how could he say no?

He tossed his soft-top carryon bag into the trunk and roared out of the airport, heading south on Interstate 10. Horace, not wanting to be pulled over by a state trooper, kept the Viper to eighty mph – only five miles per hour over! Once Google Maps told him to turn south on Highway 93, he thought, *This looks like the secondary highways back home! Let's see what this car can do!* Google Maps insisted that the speed was fifty-five mph. *Yeah, right*, thought Horace, *not when you're driving a Viper SRT10!* Speeding south, music blasting out through the speakers, he ignored a seemingly deserted settlement, just another ghost town he thought! Horace failed to see the gray Tahoe peeking out from a copse of green ash trees.

Instantly, red flashing lights came on behind the Viper. Cursing, Horace geared down and pulled over. The Tahoe pulled up slowly behind the idling car. Horace reached over for the rental documentation. A tall, slim-built man emerged from the Tahoe, adjusting his hat to cover his eyes. He approached the cooling car with a hand on his gun. This cop was taking no chances. Horace put a smile on his face, trying to be a friendly Canadian tourist.

"Sir," said the cop, his Louisiana accent making English sound like a foreign language, "do you know how fast you were traveling through our quiet little town?"

Horace failed to keep the astonished look from his face. When he caught the nameplate which read, Opie Poisson, he laughed before he could stop himself! Bad move.

"You think speeding is funny?" Anger tinged the cop's words.

"No, sir," Horace replied. "I just got caught up with the incredible sound system in this car! This is the first time I have driven a Viper. I am sorry; I guess I just got carried away."

"I clocked you going one hundred and fifty mph in a thirty-five-mph zone!"

Horace noticed the cop's indifference to the sports car. He put on his most apologetic face and said, "I am so sorry, officer!" He knew he was getting a speeding ticket. *I hope they take Mastercard*, he thought sourly.

"Sir, license and registration, please."

Horace handed over the documentation. His license was under a fake name. It was solid unless the FBI were checking it out. That is one thing Carlos did well. Deputy Opie Poisson took the documentation back to his Tahoe.

However, what happened next was something Horace never expected!

The deputy quickly marched back to the Viper and tossed the documentation through the open driver's window! Like in a Western, he drew his Glock 17 with unexpected speed and aimed it right at Horace. He barked, "Sir, shut off the car! Keep your hands visible and slowly get out of the car! Now!"

Looking at the 9mm aimed at his head, there was no choice. There was no further discussion. Horace did as he was told. Once out of the car, he heard the next order barked out, "Turn around and place your hands, palms down, on the roof. Spread your legs apart!"

Goddamn French, Goddamn Louisiana, Goddamn Carlos! Horace worked hard at keeping his anger under control. He couldn't believe his incredible bad luck. A cop with a loaded gun pointing at you less than two feet away was someone you don't want to further aggravate. He felt a cold piece of steel clamp tightly around his wrist. With a force that was surprising for such a scrawny man Horace's right arm was wrenched down and twisted behind his back. His left arm instantly followed, to be connected by this band of cold steel. Handcuffed!

Horace thought, *Now that is a first!*

"Walk to my Tahoe," came a somewhat less hostile tone. "Stop," came the next order as they approached the back door. The deputy opened the door. "Get in." Horace obliged, and the door slammed shut.

Shit, Horace thought, *I am going to be late meeting Carlos. I am sure the Sheriff will put this asshole in his place.*

What a shitty way to treat tourists! These thoughts only slightly eased Horace's increasing apprehension.

The town they entered would be complimented if it was called 'abandoned'. Horace had seen ghost towns with more people! The deputy pulled in front of a red-brick building that would have been modern two hundred years ago. Today, it was defying gravity! The Tahoe's back door was opened, and the command given. Horace got out. Together, they walked into the building.

They entered a small room with bars on the windows. On the wall opposite the door was a gun rack – four rifles standing upright like soldiers at attention. Flanking the rifles on the right were several different handguns, including a Walther PPK, a Glock, a Smith & Wesson K22, a Magnum (Horace was sure that was the one used by *Dirty Harry*), a Colt, a Luger, a Browning Hi-Power, and a Remington WP 100. Ammunition lined shelves next to the rifles and the handguns. Closed cupboards must have held other treasures – Horace would have loved the chance to check that out, but this wasn't the time or place to ask for a tour!

There was a huge man sitting behind a very large oak desk. He must have weighed in at three hundred pounds, and most of it muscle. His neck was almost absent, making his head look like it was fused to his shoulders. His hair was cut so short that it was almost colorless. His skin was red – too much sun, perhaps. The nameplate on his desk read, Colt Luger.

"Sheriff," the deputy importantly stated, "I clocked this man going 150 miles per hour! Can you believe that?"

Colt Luger slowly got up while making tuh, tuh sounds with his tongue. Seriousness permeated from him like heat waves off pavement.

"Son, you are in a hell of a lot of trouble! We take speeding very seriously."

"May I make a phone call?"

"No! This is a speeding offense, boy, not murder!" the sheriff barked.

Horace stood looking at the sheriff, expecting more to come. He couldn't help it. He asked, "Well, sir, what happens next?"

Ignoring the question, the sheriff asked, "Where are you going in such a hurry?"

"I am meeting some friends to go deep-sea fishing on Dauphin Island."

"That is too rich for my blood," the sheriff commented with a chuckle. The chuckle was quickly replaced with a scowl in his next statement. "Those Goddamn sports cars should all be sent to the crushers!"

Horace knew he was going to experience a shakedown of epic proportions. How high would the fine be? Opie nodded his head in agreement.

"I am going to fine you for speeding and driving with undue care and attention." The sheriff once more returned to his leather office chair. He grabbed a much-used soft-covered blue book off his desk and opened it. He appeared to be studying it as if he was looking for the specific fine. Horace believed this was for show. *He is watching me. How nervous do I appear? I am struggling to maintain my Canadian humbleness, although it is getting harder.*

The sheriff finally looked up and stated that the fine was one hundred ninety-two dollars, American."

Horace stood there, stunned. He thought it was going to be ten times that! "Do you take Mastercard?" he asked. The sheriff stared at him as if he had just spat on his floor. "Do you take Visa?"

"No, sir," Colt Luger indignantly announced.

"I don't have that much cash!"

The sheriff and his deputy replied together, "We do not accept cash, Mastercard, Visa, or e-transfer!"

"Then how?"

Chuckling, Deputy Opie explained, "We only accept labor."

"The 'soul of the sluggard craves and gets nothing, while the soul of the diligent is richly supplied.' Proverbs 13:4," added Sheriff Luger, nodding his head. "That's the problem with people today," he drawled. His chemically enhanced arm muscles strained at his immaculate uniform's sleeves. "Everyone thinks they can buy their way out of trouble! No siree, Bob! God honest work is your only salvation. Work is our only currency!"

Horace asked again if he could phone his friend to let him know he was going to arrive a couple of days late for the fishing trip. The only response was Opie grabbing his handcuffed hands and escorting him to a jail cell in the basement.

At the end of the first ten-hour day of clearing broken trees from an earlier storm, Horace calculated that he had earned over seventy dollars.

Another couple of days and he'd be on his way out of this shithole.

The deputy returned Horace to his cell and locked it. "Here is what you earned today," said Opie, as he handed Horace an itemized expense sheet. Lodging, three meals and each drink of water he had during the day were subtracted from the day's earnings of seventy-one dollars. His net earnings at the end of day one was fifty cents!

"What the f...? I'm in jail, not a Super-8!"

"Next time you curse, that will be a deduction of one dollar," the deputy added. "Good night. I'll be back at five with your breakfast."

After a week with no word from Horace, Carlos started his search. It was incredibly easy to follow the Viper's trek down Interstate 10. Sightings of this flashy red car speeding along became the topic of choice at many truckers' stops. The Viper was flying down Highway 93. It was then he heard about a sheriff who hated rich assholes. Carlos had found his car and Horace.

Horace was dozing off when Deputy Opie opened his cell and ordered, "Come."

"Where? Why?"

"The sheriff wants to see you, now!"

The door opened, revealing Carlos and the sheriff. "Horace, I see you had a misunderstanding with the sheriff here. I am happy to say that we have cleared up this confusion," said Carlos.

The sheriff, red with anger, said, "You are free to go, but don't let me see you again in my town."

Once outside, they quickly walked to their parked vehicles. Horace couldn't wait any longer. "What the fuck, Carlos? How did you get me out?"

"The sheriff owed me; and now you owe me, my friend!" Today, Carlos had called in his IOU.

Horace turned his attention to the babbling caller on the phone. "I charge triple for a doe and fawn." Horace stood in the early-morning dawn, angrily wondering how he ever got to this point in his life. If only he'd been with Cathy when they were both young.

"No problem!" said the voice on the phone after a moment of silence.

"That is for each," Horace said, while hoping the price would be too high.

"It is so important to me that I will even pay a price that is inflated above all reason. I want it done without any mistakes. I want it done sooner rather than later." The voice had taken on a cold tone, no longer subservient.

"Mail the information to the box number in the magazine. I will get back to you." Horace disconnected as his caller started talking.

You know what you're good for? Nothing! Horace could still hear his father's drunken voice taunting him from the grave. *Yeah, well, guess I was good for something, you old bastard – I sent you straight to Hell, didn't I?*

Hatred still burned throughout his body whenever he thought of his father.

"Who was that?" my voice sounded from behind him.

Horace jumped, guilt flushing his face. Damn, that woman moves too silently. Worry creased his face as he turned to the woman he desired and now the woman that he would lose forever if she had heard the whole conversation.

"Business," Horace said, putting his phone back into his jeans pocket.

"At this time of night, or is it morning?" I knew I sounded skeptical, thanks to my omnipresent investigative voice. "Are you hiding something from me?" I tried to make this question as innocuous as possible and pasted a smile on my face, hoping it would not look as fake as it felt.

Laughing, Horace replied, "No, sweetheart, it's business." Seeing that I was still not satisfied with this generic reason, he added, "It's an American hunter who wants me to take him big game hunting. They're always forgetting the difference in the time zones." Instantly, Horace saw something strange in my eyes. Was it disappointment? Didn't I believe him? "What's wrong?"

"I'm surprised that you're involved in hunting after that hunting trip we had when we were kids. I thought you'd never hunt again. I know I could never pick up a gun to shoot to kill. That is why I dropped out of the RCMP."

"This is a necessary supplement to my farming income," Horace snapped. "Farming doesn't always pay the bills." He regretted saying these words as soon as they were out of his mouth. *Christ, why can't there be a Control Z to instantly take back spoken words?*

I involuntarily took a step back. "I'm going to get dressed. It's time for me to go home."

"Shit!" Horace hoarsely whispered to my departing back as I walked into the master bedroom, softly closing the door behind me. He remained standing in the empty semi-dark room, hating his life and his father.

***

Horace and I never returned to discussing his other job as a big game hunting guide. During the following week before Horace was to fly into the States, we went out every night. The feelings we had as teenagers had not left us; rather, they had lain dormant in our hearts until now, when they were awakened. Our shared feelings, our shared attractions were blossoming with adult desires and passions. I still experienced feelings of guilt over my involvement with Horace. I couldn't get rid of a nagging thought that it was too soon to become involved with another man, even one I had known since I was a kid. This concern was highlighted more when my mother continually compared Horace to Geoff, with Horace always ending up superior. I struggled with my anger. I wanted to yell out that Geoff was a terrific guy, a criminal reporter who gave up his life to expose some insane murderer in this area, in her area. He was so close to exposing one of her dear neighbors as a serial killer!

My thoughts of Horace and Geoff continued to merge and separate in my mind. Each man was able to make me feel so complete, so fulfilled, so much more beautiful, when I knew I was far, far removed from physical gorgeousness. I understood why men in some parts of the world had kept harems for their multiple wives, because right now I had two men I loved equally yet differently. Was I practicing psychological polygamy?

No! I knew in my heart that if Geoff were still alive, I would never have given Horace a second thought. Today, without Geoff's love, I knew that I was totally committed to Horace, and was beginning to think in terms of life-long, like the rest of my life. I knew this blossoming love was based on neither my teenage crush nor on my physical yearning for Geoff. I knew it was real and special for Horace, a deep affection which was separate from my eternal love for Geoff.

The ringing of my phone woke me. Half asleep and thinking it was Horace, I rolled over in bed to grab my cell phone. "Hello," I said dreamily into the phone, thinking of Horace lying naked in his bed, talking to me on his phone. The early-morning sun would be shining on his suntanned, toned body.

"Cathy, is that you?" a familiar voice tentatively asked.

"Oh, hi, Lou, I'm sorry, I was asleep!" I said, embarrassment washing over me, heating my body, reddening my face.

"I was phoning to see how your story is coming, as you haven't sent anything in yet," Lou continued, once more all business-like.

I had returned to Saskatoon after being home for a few days and took Geoff's story to Lou. I had asked him if he would let me continue where Geoff had left off. At first, he had refused, citing the obvious danger; but soon, with my many arguments in favor of me doing this story, Lou's old investigative reporter instinct took over and he reluctantly gave in to my request. Lou had known the potential of this exposé – if it could be completed.

"I will e-mail you what I have right after I make coffee," I answered, getting out of bed and pulling on my jeans and a sweatshirt.

"How much time do you think you'll need before you come back?" asked Lou.

"I think another month, maybe six weeks," I said.

"Fine, but no more than six weeks. If you don't have the story by then, well then, there is no story. Understood?" Lou's voice reflected his concern.

"Thanks, Lou, that seems fair," I said as I walked into the kitchen.

"Who was that, dear?" asked Mom. She was wearing the last housecoat Dad had given to her before he died. It was threadbare and hung on her small frame, making her appear frailer than I had remembered.

"It was my boss asking when I was coming back to work. It seems I am missed. I must e-mail Lou as to where a certain file is. I couldn't remember when we were talking, but I just thought of how I filed it." I knew talking about being a secretary would lose Mom's attention very quickly. It did.

"Fine, I'll make coffee. What do you want for breakfast? Hot or cold?" asked Mom as she busied herself with the coffee preparation.

"Cold is fine," I said, as sadness draped over me as loosely as Mom's housecoat with her lack of interest in my job. I left the kitchen to e-mail my progress to Lou.

Shortly after breakfast, I took Mom's grocery list and left for Keysound. Mom had also wanted to go into Sourtaw, which was in the opposite direction. She was not up to doing both towns today, so I took Keysound. Something was pushing me in that direction. What? Instinct? Geoff?

I was about a mile down the road when I saw a lone small figure standing on the edge of the road, frantically waving his hands. I slowed, as was the custom of the area, neighbors helping neighbors. I thought about what happened to Geoff, exposed on the highway. *If the killer knows what you're up to, this would be a great scenario*, my logical voice cautioned, *and you won't even hear the shot*. Involuntarily, I shuddered and gripped the wheel harder as my foot eased down on the brake.

"Missy, am I ever glad to see you," called Tyrell as I rolled to a stop. He hurried to my opened passenger window and continued to talk. "I... er, my truck broke down, it died, and I need a ride into town. Can you oblige me?" he asked, and a mixture of liquor scents on his breath drifted into my car.

"Okay, get in," I said, wondering if Tyrell ever quit drinking. His hair was entangled as if it hadn't seen a comb in months. His face reflected the waiflike body slowly being embalmed by liquor. His face hosted a thin, grey speckled, scraggly beard, a beard that had been growing for weeks.

Tyrell hurriedly opened the Mustang's passenger door and seemingly poured his frame onto the leather bucket seat. "I am lucky that you were the one to stop and not..." He paused as his hands began to tremble as he attempted to do up his seatbelt.

I leaned over to help him. Tyrell's hands were shaking uncontrollably. I grabbed the seatbelt and inserted it into its slot. With the sound of the click came a small, "Thanks," from his direction.

We drove silently for a few minutes. Tyrell seemed very nervous. "Tyrell, what were you going to say back there?" I asked when he didn't finish his sentence.

"Huh? Missy?" Tyrell looked baffled at my request.

I decided to approach this a different way and said, "Tyrell, you know most of the people around here. Do you think you catch wind of what goes on?"

"Missy, I know about everything that goes on here," he said. A feeling of self-importance made him sit straighter than before. In a stronger, more confident voice, he added, "I know who is good, like your family, and who is evil, like..." Here he paused, suddenly sensing danger. He furtively looked about my car, fear evident in his face. Tyrell hugged his bony frame and looked straight ahead.

"Tyrell, you said my family is good, and I thank you. However, you can tell me about anything that is going on here that is strange. If you tell me about a friend, I promise I won't get angry and I will never tell another person," I said, sincerity strong in my voice. I was not sure why I added the part about a friend, but my investigative reporter's instincts were firmly planted in the driver's seat for this conversation.

Tyrell looked at me as I drove. He thought about this for several seconds. I was beginning to think that this was a dead end, when he began his story.

"I like you, missy," Tyrell said, his watery cognac brown eyes staring at me, wavering as they continually focused then refocused my face into view. "You are intelligent," Tyrell started, "and inquisitive," he finished.

Somehow, the wisdom in his words was as out of character for Tyrell as was his wearing a tux or his being sober!

Uncertain as to what I should say, fearful of scaring him from talking, I said, slightly smiling, "Hmmm."

I continued to drive slowly down this lonely country road. The only company out here were the myriad assortment of bugs smearing their insides across the windshield. Tyrell took this as a signal to continue.

"Why did you come back here after all these years?" Tyrell asked, the watery, bloodshot eyes flittering over my face, avoiding my eyes.

"I have come back for visits, you know," I said, suddenly feeling defensive. I knew that I should have come home more often.

"Now don't get me wrong, Missy," said Tyrell, "I think it is good that you date our local boys." His conversation took yet another sharp turn into an area I was not prepared to discuss, especially with Tyrell.

I shot him a look that said, *Watch it!* This was missed by Tyrell, who seemed unaware of my uneasiness as he adjusted his scrawny ass in the soft black leather bucket seat.

"But" – another pause as he adjusted his seatbelt – "well, Missy, is it all right that I call you Missy?" he asked, once more going off on yet another tangent.

"Sure it is all right, Tyrell," I said, my voice reflecting some of my exasperation. We drove on in silence. My logical inquisitive voice hissed, *There you go, Missy, you have gone and frightened him. Investigative reporter? Humph!* My spirit sank even lower with Tyrell's next words.

"The crops sure are good this year," said Tyrell, "as long as we don't get an early frost."

What would Geoff do? I asked myself. "Yes, you are quite correct!" I said softly, removing the earlier agitation from my voice. Fearing that Tyrell would begin to wander off on another digression, I casually brought up the killing, just like Tyrell brought up the crops. "I love the country. I think the reason why is because it is so very safe here! You don't get the crime we get in the cities, the burglaries, the armed robberies, the murders." My words hung in the car for a few seconds.

"Safe? Phooey!" loudly snorted Tyrell. "It wasn't safe for that reporter who was nosing around here a short time back!"

The mention of Geoff caused me to involuntarily jerk the steering wheel. "Missy, watch where you're going!" Tyrell said, nervously looking back at the road. "What's the matter?" he asked.

"Didn't you see that rabbit?" I asked, hoping he wouldn't catch me in the lie. "I swerved around it to miss it!"

"Rabbit? I didn't see any dang rabbit!" Tyrell snorted.

"Tyrell, you were looking at me, so how could you have seen a rabbit or anything on the road?" I asked, allowing a little indignation to color my words. In doing so, I hoped for a more honest flavor.

"I will watch the road more carefully," Tyrell said gravely. "It is very important to watch out for anything on the road, but a rabbit!" he added derisively. "Women! Don't you know you can just run the dang thing over? Won't hurt your car any, hurt him more." Tyrell laughed at his joke. His laugh sounded very much like an unvoiced snort followed by a chuff which repeated several times, each time a little louder.

Faking my own chuckle, I said, "Thanks, Tyrell." I then pressed him for the story he had started. "Tyrell, I am very sorry for interrupting you when you began to tell me about the stranger who had come into town. It was a woman nosing around, you said." I was deliberately choosing a woman as I wanted him to think that I was only listening out of politeness.

"Missy, if you are going to listen as badly as you drive, then I am going to just sit here and watch the road with you," Tyrell said, his voice reflecting hurt feelings from too many years of ridicule. Looking at the hurt reflected in his eyes staring at me, I remembered that long-ago doe. The same feeling of protectiveness suddenly washed over me. I felt strangely akin to this man, this town drunk who lived in a fifth of rye, yet this man was proving to have a wisdom that many would have never recognized.

"Sorry, Tyrell, I will do better at both jobs, listening and watching the road!" I said, laughing lightly as I attempted to lighten the black mood that had suddenly settled over us. I slowed down even more, wanting to prolong the trip into town. Tyrell took this decrease in speed as a signal that I would be more attentive to both the road as well as his story that he appeared eager to tell.

"It was a reporter, like I had said," began Tyrell, "but it was a man, not a woman. Women aren't reporters!" Tyrell snorted at the absurdity of a woman being a reporter. I smiled at his outdated chauvinism. Surprisingly, Tyrell and Lou had something in common. "He was here looking into

the disappearances of different people. Some were locals."
Tyrell paused, thinking. "Some were visitors to the area."

"What do you mean by visitors?"

"Visitors!" Tyrell said loudly, annoyed at my naivety.
"You know, hunters, tourists, those kinds of visitors!"

"Sorry, Tyrell, please go on. I promise not to ask any
silly questions."

"That's okay, Missy," Tyrell replied, his voice softening.
"After all, you are just a woman. Things like this are hard for
females to understand!" I hid my laughter in a cough and
Tyrell continued.

"You know, it is midmorning and I haven't had breakfast
yet!" Tyrell said, snapping his fingers so loudly that he made
me jump. "Breakfast is the most important meal of the day."
His voice was soft, childlike. "Yep, that is what my momma
always said!" he ended with conviction.

Smiling at his obvious hinting, I offered, "Why, Tyrell,
why don't we go to the café and have a bite in Keysound? I
haven't had breakfast yet," I lied, "and I was planning on
having toast and coffee. I would love to have company; that
is, if you don't have any pressing engagements." I smiled my
most innocent smile at Tyrell. He looked out the windshield.
Keysound was looming in the distance. We would be pulling
into town in a few minutes, even traveling at thirty-five miles
per hour. Silence was greeted by the sound of the wheels on
the gravel road. Just as I was beginning to think that this
approach was too bold, and a new tactic would be in order,
Tyrell broke the silence.

"Well, Missy, since we're both going for breakfast, let's
eat together. I eat alone most of the time and I would like a

pretty filly like you to join me!" Tyrell had lowered his voice and looked about the car, expecting some demon to jump out and devour him.

"You have a date!" I replied pleasantly. My mind was already at work as to how to learn his story, his knowledge about Geoff's murder.

The Double Bar restaurant was the best place to eat in town, as well as the only place to eat! The outside was finished in treated wood and red brick. Wagon wheels outlined the deck, where several tables were placed for patrons to eat at. Half wagon wheels were partially buried in the soil, forming a fence outlining the sidewalk leading up to the screen door. Tyrell moved quickly ahead of me and opened the door, saying, "Ladies first!"

Laughing, I thanked him. Standing beside a 'Please wait to be seated' sign, I suggested eating outside in the beautiful sunshine. Tyrell eagerly agreed. The waitress arrived as if on cue and asked inside or outside. "Outside," we said together. She gave me a quizzical look and a demeaning glance at Tyrell. In one swift, smooth motion she turned, grabbed two plastic-coated menus, and started walking toward the outside deck. We quickly followed behind her.

"Service seems to be very fast here!" I commented to Tyrell as the waitress brusquely brought us to a corner table on the deck and slapped the two menus down.

Chuckling, Tyrell said, "Service is always fast when you are with me. You see, they want me gone as quickly as possible!"

"That is mean!" I said indignantly.

"Nah, they don't mean anything by it," countered Tyrell. "I know I am a drunk, I can't hold a job, and I am a joke." His thin, bloodless lips smiled. "However," he chuckled, "I have brought fun to other people's lives. Guess that gives me an important job after all!" Here was a man considered as unimportant and worthless by society but was humble in his forgiveness of their cruel treatment of him. Tyrell was a man who was knowledgeable of life's treacherous personalities, schemes, and motives, but, ironically, without the knowledge of many living in the local communities!

The overweight waitress returned before we had a chance to look at our menus. Tyrell, seeming accustomed to the treatment, said, "Bring me two eggs, two pieces of toast and coffee. Make my eggs sunny side up and bring honey for my toast. Don't want any jam!" Smiling, Tyrell turned to look expectantly at me.

"Toast and coffee, honey for my toast as well. Toast on brown bread, please."

"Same here," quickly added Tyrell.

"Humph!" was blown out of the waitress' pursed lips as she leaned over the tabletop, picking up the menus.

We sat alone outside, listening to some birds chirping. Their music seemed to relax Tyrell. He leaned back in his chair and smiled up at the sun. "The thing I am going to miss when I'm gone are the birds' songs!" Tyrell said in a voice full of sincerity but without any sadness about the unfairness of life. A truck with a noisy muffler rambled down the road. Its presence made Tyrell nervous. He cautiously looked around and lowered his voice. "You know, Missy, you never know when someone is listening. In a small community it is sometimes dangerous to be overheard!" Astonishingly, Tyrell winked at me!

"Tyrell, this is not a movie!" I said, keeping my voice lowered. "This is Keysound, where nothing happens!" I said, laughing lightly. My investigative reporter's instinct was on high alert. Could this be the very person who would solve Geoff's murder and allow me to finish his story? My eagerness was pressing as hard as a flooding river against a sandbag dike.

The waitress, who was on the other side of fifty, returned, setting down two steaming mugs of coffee. She turned and quickly left – a drill sergeant would have been impressed with her about-face turn! A freight train came noisily through town, its horn blowing as it neared the railway crossing. Its wheels rumbled on the tracks. Ripples appeared on the surface of the coffee in our big, solid mugs. With the disappearance of the train, the bleached blonde waitress appeared with our breakfast plates.

"Anything else?" asked the waitress, directing the question at me.

Looking at Tyrell, who shook his head no, I replied, smiling, "No, thanks, that will be all!"

Tyrell picked up the small packet of honey and emptied it into his coffee. Not surprisingly, he took out a silver flask and poured some of its light brown liquid into his coffee as well. Sipping the coffee, a smile spread across his lips. "They don't know I do this! You know this place is not licensed! I guess I pulled one over them!" Tyrell didn't wait for me to applaud his craftiness. He started to wolf down his breakfast. Between eating and swallowing, Tyrell advised, "Eat, Missy, or it'll get cold!"

I obeyed and ate in silence, wondering how to get him to return to the subject of the murdered reporter. I didn't have to wait long. With the last piece of toast and egg in his mouth, Tyrell wiped his mouth off and downed the rest of his own special blend of coffee. "You know, Missy, that was not right, the killing of that young man! I liked him, ya' know! He talked to me and listened, kinda like what you're doing. He treated me like I was important!" Tyrell paused, thinking back to his last meeting with Geoff. "George Adams was his name, Missy, a real nice young man. Yeah, he was just doing what the cops should have been doing all along. Smarter than them, maybe too smart for his own britches!"

My heart lurched at hearing such praise of Geoff from this unlikely person. Tears threatened to betray me, so I took a sip of coffee and brought them under control quickly, keeping them from dripping out of my eyes.

"You know he wanted to know about the disappearances and possible killings that are going on around here. I told him that the rumors were correct, as I had seen one of the killings!"

I gasped out, "My God, Tyrell! Why didn't you go to the police?" My palms were wet with sweat; my heart threatened cardiac arrest.

"Police! Do you really think they would listen to me? They would just laugh at me and probably lock me up for being drunk. Some were in cahoots with him, too!" Leaning forward on his elbows, he continued, "I never had the chance to tell George the name of the killer before that miserable excuse of a human killed George. But you know, Missy, I am old. I won't live forever, might even die today. I don't want to go to meet my Maker with this on my conscience." Tyrell's voice took on a tone of new urgency, as if he was in imminent danger. "The killer is someone you know, Missy." He looked at me, his gaze no longer watery and wavering, his eyes appearing focused and intense. "Don't get mad at me."

"Go on, Tyrell, I won't be mad no matter what you tell me. I promise, cross my heart, hope to…"

"No!" Tyrell yelled, grabbing my hand as I started to cross my heart, jerking it down to the tabletop, stopping me dead. He quickly lowered his voice. "Don't say that! I don't want you killed – and when I tell you his name, you are in the same danger as George Adams!"

"Sorry," I said softly.

"His name was…" Tyrell paused and again checked out to see if anyone was listening. He leaned closer to me. I could see his stained teeth, smell coffee and Jack Daniels on his breath, mingled with the odors from a mouth that had not seen a toothbrush or a dentist in a very long time. Fighting an impulse to gag from this smell of decay, I held his gaze with all the strength I could muster. "The killer and the murderer of George Adams is—" he paused then said, "Horace!"

The waitress' sudden return with the meal bill stopped and looked at my frozen shocked face. Slowly I looked up at her.. "Are you paying by cash or with credit card?" Her eyes stared at me with a disapproving glare. *Is she thinking I'm letting Tyrell come on to me?* I almost laughed out loud. I was not able to stop my lips from slightly curling upward into a smile.

"Visa," I replied.

"You'll have to come to the till," the waitress said, waiting for me to stand up and follow her.

"Thank you, Missy," Tyrell said in a low voice as he rose and shuffled toward the door. "Please be careful."

I was suddenly fearful for his life remembering his words that it can be dangerous to be overheard. I said, "Any time you're out and about, just flag me down and we can go for coffee or a meal!" Tyrell turned back to me, smiling, and walked out of the restaurant. I followed the waitress to the cash register and paid for our meals, offering the scowling waitress a dollar tip. I was tempted to tip her a penny, but my manners stopped me. A dollar or a penny, she didn't deserve either tip.

The more pressing problem was how I could casually bump into Tyrell in the next day or so? I needed more information, more details. I had to find out what Tyrell had told Geoff. My blood was surging through my veins at being so close to the answer! *Geoff*, my heart cried, *soon, honey, you'll have justice!* Unsuppressed tears were dripping out of my eyes as I walked back to my car.

Now

"There, there, don't cry, dearie." A soft, cool hand pats my bare arm.

"Lou just left for dinner."

Slowly, I open my eyes. I see my personal nurse. What is her name?

My thoughts are bouncing about in my head and the resulting pain spurs more tears to flow.

"Do you remember my name?" she asks.

I scream to myself, *Why can't I remember the name of the person who is always here when I wake up?* Suddenly, a video of two women in a chocolate factory picking out chocolates that were not formed correctly starts to play in my mind. Increasing numbers of imperfect chocolates come along the constantly moving assembly line belt. The red-haired person starts eating them, then she begins to stuff them into her shirt, her pockets... "*I Love Lucy*," I breathe out, smiling.

"I love you, too, dearie," Lucy replies, smiling at my success. "Is there anything you need? How's your pain level? Any discomfort?"

"No to everything," I answer. I am feeling an inane amount of pride at remembering her name.

"Your pain is tolerable?"

"Yes," I chuckle, "I have brothers! I can tolerate a lot of pain!"

"Rest. You've had a very good day. You deserve a break."

"At McDonald's!" I sing slightly off-key.

Laughing, Lucy walks out of my draped-in hospital room. I notice that the hospital sounds are muted. *Evening*, my analytical voice announces. "Yes," I sigh, rolling over onto my side. My eyes close and all sounds quickly fade to black.

Then

"Whoa!" Horace growled into his sat phone. "Say that again." His blood began to run cold as he listened to the caller. "Okay, okay!" he said, his voice menacing.

"Does this mean that I'll get the same amount as last time? This is good info, yeah?" a small, tinny, whiny voice came from the phone's speaker.

"Same," Horace said, and abruptly ended the call just as the voice started to speak. Like the old man always said, *Boy, don't trust women. Women are born to fuck you!* Horace could still hear his father's cold laugh. Horace knew that he had to finish this hunting trip now. There was no more time to waste on the wisdom of what he was about to do. He had unfinished business to take care of when he returned home. Anger riled up his stomach acid. He felt the acid moving up his throat, burning it as it progressed to his mouth. He grabbed a couple of extra strength Gaviscon antacid tablets and slowly ground them between his teeth.

Lovingly, he lifted a Finnish-built rifle, his father's 7.62 TKIV 85, and smoothly slid the 7.62 X 53mm bullet home. Horace breathed in, then out, slowing his heartbeat while unbidden and unwanted thoughts were whirling around, banging off the inside of his skull. *Fuck, fuck, fuck*, his mind yelled, anger ripping through his chest. *Goddamn Carlos! Goddamn Tyrell!*

Clear your head, boy, long-dead Floyd's voice snarled in his head.

Horace took another cleansing breath and then he looked through his Vortex Viper PST 4 -16x riflescope. Still not steady enough, slight movement.

Don't waste the shot, cautioned his brain. He breathed in slowly, then exhaled slowly. All unwanted thoughts were fading with each exhalation. His mind was clearing. He rehearsed his movements. Chamber the bullet and aim the Dane, his name for the well-used rifle, at the toddler when she was at the apex of backward swing. Her small body would be in alignment with her mother's head. One bullet, two kills. Neither would feel pain.

Neither would be afraid. Neither would see the other die.

Patiently, he observed the young woman pushing a toddler on a swing in a deserted park. He was told that the mother routinely brought her daughter out at noon when most other mothers and kids are home enjoying lunch.

The toddler, a little girl with red hair flying about in the breeze, laughed as her mother pushed her. "Harder," cried the little girl. *Push*, the toddler flew away from her mother, and just as the toddler reached her apex, her swing rushed back towards her mother. This motion elicited a joyful laugh from both the child and her mother.

Horace followed the motion. *Push*, wait for the swing to come back, then push again. Feel the rhythm. *Push*, wait for the swing to come back, then push again. Breathe in, breathe out. Feel the rhythm. He aimed his Dane. He waited till the toddler was level with her mother. He pressed the trigger once. The bullet tore through the toddler's chest and into the mother's head. The bullet continued to travel through the park, losing velocity until it hit a tree trunk, embedding itself. Meanwhile, the dead toddler flew into her mother, who was missing her face. Together, they landed on the ground, the swing continuing to swing back and forth, slowing until it came to rest.

Horace phoned the preprogrammed number and growled, "Debt paid." He pulled out the SIM card and snapped it in half. The battery was removed. He put the pieces into his pocket. He would deposit a piece at a time on his way to the airport. He packed his Dane into a specially constructed six-foot upright double bass instrument. Lovingly, he set the replicated instrument that looked like a cello on steroids into a large and well-used lightweight hard-sided travel case. He latched the case and locked the two combination locks, securing it for its flight back home in luggage. He raised up like a specter of death, carrying the case away from the kill site to his rental parked nearby.

His flight leaves in three hours.

***

Sleep, once my friend that offered me a respite from the harsh realities of life, abandoned me. Each night I revisited my breakfast with Tyrell.

Leaning closer to Tyrell to hear who had killed Geoff. *Someone you know; Horace* his words kept echoing inside my head.

Tyrell was afraid of Horace. Horace, on the other hand, dismissed Tyrell with the same disgust he'd have when finding a wood tick biting his arm. Or perhaps Tyrell was a troublemaker, a fabricator of stories spun for a free meal; or was he the real thing?

My logical self argued that I should not dismiss Tyrell as unreliable.

Tyrell's hushed voice replayed in my mind: *George Adams was his name, Missy, a real nice young man. Yeah, he was just doing what the cops should have been doing all along. Smarter than them, maybe too smart for his own britches!* "All right, enough!" I whispered in my sleep as I continued to toss and turn.

You did see the coldness in Horace's eyes in the bar, my analytical voice reminded me. *It was there for just a nanosecond, don't you remember?* Words from my heart came in to soothe my suspicions. *Horace just wanted to be with you; he didn't want to share you. That is so romantic!*

An unbidden thought crept in, suggesting that I should talk to Horace as soon as he returned from his hunting trip. *Hunting?* my investigative voice challenged. *It's not hunting season anywhere.* Horace's deep, sexy voice soothed this query. I recalled his face, his smile as he told me that it is always hunting season somewhere in the world! *Humph! And you call yourself an investigative reporter?* my logical voice scoffed. I had to learn the hard way to take my analytical voice much more seriously.

Had Tyrell told me that Floyd Moonie was the murderer I could readily accept that, hands down. Didn't he abuse his kids? Or perhaps his crazy wife? She had killed her son, a wee baby, for Christ sake! My practical voice countered with a question that stopped all arguments. *Floyd is dead and his wife is in the old folks' home confined to a wheelchair, so who killed Geoff?*

My investigative reporter's voice inside of me won this round hands down! A feeling of apprehension and dread like a blanket was folding around my heart. It started to squeeze my heart. Tighter and tighter. Soon, I began to find it hard to take a deep breath. Sickeningly, I realized that my future was no longer mine to control; rather, I was spiraling out of control towards an end that I instinctively feared.

Tears of hurt and betrayal bubbled out of my eyes. Was I so ready to convict Horace? Whatever happened to keeping an open mind? Would I really be making love to Geoff's killer? To a serial killer? Peacefulness finally calmed my restless sleep when I promised myself that I would talk with Tyrell and ask him for proof. No more dancing around. I needed facts. I needed names, places and dates.

***

"Cathy!" Mom's voice shattered my short-lived sleep. "Cathy, are you awake? Horace is on the phone!"

"I'm awake now," I grumbled. "What time is it?" I asked as I sat up in my childhood bed, rubbing sleep from my eyes. I felt that I had just drifted off to sleep minutes ago. I had to start getting more sleep.

"Why, it's eight; the day's half gone!" Mom's cheerful reply came.

"Yeah, I know, I know," I groggily said, putting my feet on the floor. "I couldn't sleep last night."

As I wrapped around me the plush robe that Geoff had bought, new tears threatened. Shaking my head to dismiss these sentimental, unproductive thoughts, I walked into the sunny kitchen to see Mom clutching the phone to her chest. "I think he really loves you, Cathy. Don't you let him get away!" she whispered. Mom looked so happy. My heart felt like a cold, hard rock.

"Thanks, Mom," I softly said, reaching for the phone. I knew that I would have to meet with Horace and then try to ask him about Tyrell's story without getting Tyrell into trouble. Was it possible that Horace was, because of his drunken father, merely the target of malicious lies told by a drunk who had never gotten along with the Moonies? Grasping the receiver in a trembling hand, I softly said, "Hi."

"Hi, darling!" Horace's husky, sensual voice came over the telephone line. "I was wondering if you would like to go into the city to the casino. We could make a night of it, stay at the Ramada and return tomorrow, richer from our gambling!"

"You're back from your hunting trip?" I inanely asked. "I thought you'd be gone for another few days."

"I couldn't stand being away from you any longer, so I cut it short and came home!" he said. I imagined Horace standing in his breakfast nook, foot hooked on a stool, and smiling. Would a murderer do this? Would a paid killer sound so normal?

"That sounds splendid, but..." I paused and gave Mom a look, which meant privacy. Beaming at me, she took her coffee and left the kitchen, humming. Alone in the kitchen, I mustered up the sexiest voice I was able to create. How could my heart continue to beat? I felt dead on the inside.

Tenderly, I said in a hushed voice, "Horace, I don't feel like sharing you with people tonight. I want you all to myself tonight."

Chuckling, Horace added, "Ah, my wanton vixen! This is what I love about you, you are so unpredictable. I love the way you keep me on my toes! I can never guess what you are going to say or do! Pick you up after supper, about eight?"

Surprised, I asked, "Why not now?"

"Darling," he drawled, "I have some work to do today! I should be done by eight, maybe seven thirty."

"I guess I will just have to wait," I said, disappointment dripping from my voice. Hanging up the phone, I wondered what type of job he would have to do today. He had just returned from his hunting trip. His farm was grain, not livestock. He was an organic farmer, so no spraying for weeds nor insects.

Fear nipped at my soul. I shivered. Had I overlooked something?

Mom reentered the kitchen, interrupting my troubling thoughts. I slowly turned to her with a big fake smile pasted on my face.

"Are you going out tonight, dear?" she asked, her face beaming with happiness!

"Yeah, about seven thirty."

"Good, we can actually have supper together," Mom said. "I don't like eating alone!" I did not know that would be the last time I would ever see, talk to, or eat with Mom.

***

I was ready to leave by seven thirty. I was dressed in my form-fitting blue jeans (no fashionable holes in the knees; sorry, I just can't buy into that) and a dark red satin blouse with flutter sleeves. The contrast of texture distracted from my less than sexy figure. Horace seemed to enjoy my full figure, something I had to trim down! *Don't mess with perfection,* my romantic voice cooed. My investigative voice advised, *Keep his full attention on you and not on your subtle, or not so subtle, questions.*

I didn't want to make Horace suspicious. I wanted to be in control, maybe more now than ever before in my life. I had to keep my feelings, my desires in check. *If he is the killer, is he just going to say so?* my skeptical investigative reporter voice queried.

Silly, interrupted my romantic voice, *he is going to be a lady killer and tonight you are going to be ravaged to within an inch of your life!* My heart scoffed at my analytical voice.

Quit! I silently shouted. The voices ceased!

I decided that after we got to enjoy each other, pleasure before business, I would disclose to Horace the real reason I was back home. The guilt I was feeling would disperse with my full confession. Once Horace learned of Geoff's real job and why he was in this area, I felt optimistic Horace could help me solve this mystery. I wondered for the umpteenth time why I hadn't already told Horace about Geoff. Horace would probably laugh at my attempt to be an investigative reporter. I was ready – or was I really?

Horace drove into the driveway at seven thirty and I left the house quickly, preferring to get this evening underway without losing my resolve. As I hopped into his truck, Horace took my urgency as a sexual need. His hands reached out and caressed my crotch as I closed the door. "Horace," I said, blushing, "not in my driveway! My Mom is watching at the window!"

"Sorry, darling," Horace said, his voice huskier than I remembered. "I just want you so bad!" His hand returned to the steering wheel and he waited while I buckled up my seatbelt. He put his truck into reverse and backed up. He stopped and put the transmission into drive, pausing so we could wave back at my smiling mother who was now waving at us through the kitchen window. Horace turned the wheel and stepped on the gas. The truck's wheels spun on the gravel. At the road we turned right, something I had expected. *Ah, he is taking you to his house so you can enjoy each other for hours and hours*, my heart's silky voice whispered excitedly.

At least at his house you can escape if necessary, my voice of reason added. Several minutes later, Horace surprised me when he turned right, down a very narrow, treelined, dirt lane into an abandoned farmyard.

"Some place new?" I asked, hoping my voice didn't show the sudden apprehension I was feeling.

"Darling, I am taking you to my favorite place. It is very special. I have never taken another living soul here. I want

172

some place private for us. I want tonight to be a night you will never forget!"

Although his words were spoken with the same sensual passion, I felt coldness creep down my backbone. I shivered. He parked his truck on the side of the driveway beside a long-deserted stone farmhouse. Weeds were successfully competing with wildflowers and bushes for space in this abandoned yard.

Horace turned to me in his seat and possessively draped his right arm around my shoulder, caressing my right cheek and breast. I shivered again. He turned my face up to his and kissed me long and hard, his tongue erasing my feelings of trepidation. For the time being, I was again lost in his touch.

"Sweetheart," Horace said huskily, "let's get out of this truck."

Laughing, I said, "I don't see any place to move to!"

Horace reached behind my seat and pulled out a blanket. Holding the soft-looking blanket and smiling mischievously, he said, "Darling, the great outdoors awaits us!"

Our lovemaking was the most intense that I had ever experienced with Horace. Perhaps this was due to my gut feeling that I was about to lose my second love, my childhood love. Would he forgive me for my duplicity?

Horace's tongue worked between my thighs, bringing me to the brink of climax, only to retreat up my sweat-soaked belly, between my breasts and back to my mouth. Horace's hands were sending electric spasms throughout my body until I was moaning, writhing, begging for release.

Afterwards, satiated with our lovemaking, we fully enjoyed the comfort of the very thick, very soft blanket that lay between us and the hard, weedy ground. The cool night breeze caressed away our exhaustion and dried the sweat on our bodies. We stared up at the stars.

"Cathy," Horace said gruffly, breaking the silence, "I know you feel exactly like I do." Horace paused, waiting for an affirmative response from me.

"Hmm," I mumbled, pretending to be engrossed in the millions of stars above us. I waited to see where he was going with this. I was not sure how to broach Geoff's identity and his investigation. I was even less sure how I was going to admit to my underhandedness.

Horace cleared his throat and then continued, uncertainty sounding in his next words, "I want you to be with me forever, be my lover." He rolled over on his side to stare at my face in the moonlight. "Be my friend, be my wife!" Horace ended with a hungry kiss that left me breathless.

"Horace, I do love you! I have always loved you and I will continue to love you. We must always be upfront with each other." An uncomfortable silence ensued.

Horace asked, "Cathy, you remember that deer hunting trip we went on when we were kids?" I shuddered at the memory of the coldness of the kill. I welcomed his strong, warm arms when they wrapped around me.

Neither of us moved. Once more silence pressed down on us. I was afraid to speak! "Darling, I didn't realize that we were actually helping the deer population as a whole!"

I jerked away from him and sat bolt upright. The thought of Horace's touch nauseated me. I hugged my arms about my bare legs, trying to hide my trembling. "How did you come up with that idea?" I asked caustically. I recognized one of his inebriated father's gems.

"My old man told me that!" Horace said defensively. "Don't you see? If they get overpopulated, then many will starve to death. Do you think we killed the smartest deer? Well?" When I remained silent, he repeated his question, "Well?" His voice had slowly risen in volume. His words hammered at my heart. Tears brimmed my eyes. Who was this man? We are so isolated here! Terror had my heart beating double time. Should I be afraid of Horace? *Definitely!* my analytical mind screamed. *Run! Get out of here! Now!* I could only sit, paralyzed, too afraid to move!

Horace's eyes took on a light of their own and burned into me. He waited for my answer. Unable to suppress my anger, I shot back, "I don't know!" My investigative reporter's voice screamed, *Christ, don't challenge him!*

Horace's face became harder, meaner. Fear gripped my body. I decided that this was not the time to confess the real purpose for my visit home. I would not ask Horace about the killings in the area. In that moment I knew I was looking into the eyes of the serial killer, the killer for hire. I realized that I might never see home again if I didn't tamp down my temper and my disgust.

Softening my voice, I whispered, "Why are we talking about something that happened so long ago?" I forced myself to move back and sat once more beside him. I cupped his face in my hands. "Why don't we forget the past and just hold each other close?" I murmured, hoping that Horace wouldn't hear the terror in my voice. I sobbed, "I wanted this night to be memorable."

Horace held me. I hid my revulsion. "It's okay, darling, don't cry." His voice was once more like a lover's. Maybe everything would be all right. I would see home again; I'd hug my Mom and tell her that I loved her! His hands rubbed my back as he rocked me slowly in his arms. My tears subsided. My muscles relaxed.

Horace's soft voice whispered into my ear, "Darling, I want to be upfront with you." Horace seemed so sincere, like he was a teenager once more. He was once again the teenager I fell in love with. He was the man I wanted to spend the rest of my life with. He kissed me softly on my lips. "You know, darling, that humans are also part of the animal family, and just like wild animals we also have those who are weak, those who are evil and those who just drain society as a whole." Sickening premonition, like icy swamp slime, began to ooze over my heart and my soul. His softly spoken words terrified me.

Horace, feeling my body trembling in his arms, bared his teeth in a facsimile of a smile. "Darling, I have another blanket in my truck; let me get it for you. I don't want you to die from exposure!" he balefully whispered in a low, husky voice; a voice that I had only hours earlier thought to be sensual. A voice that had warmed me to my core. Now that same voice had the power to flash-freeze me like a ReJoice freezer. I smiled feebly and agreed that I was very cold. Horace rose, his naked body reflecting the soft moonlight, muscles that were so sensuous hours ago appearing as dangerous as the muscles rippling through the body of a wild mountain lion, ready to leap upon its prey – me.

"Polar opposite," said my early morning English class professor, her red, red lips drew my eyes to her. My attention was riveted to those Botox-enlarged red lips as they ceased moving and she looked directly at me expecting me to finish her definition!

"Two who are extremely opposed in their beliefs," I breathed out. Geoff and Horace are my Polar loves! I wept softly. A bullet destroyed my adult love of Geoff as it tore through his beautiful and caring heart. My childhood fantasy with Horace and I living happily ever after had imploded in this deserted, abandoned farmyard with the impact of Horace's words. As Horace moved towards his truck, I stood up and quickly dressed. My fingers were trembling as badly as if I was suffering from Parkinson's disease. I uttered a silent prayer to God and to Geoff to help me maneuver my way out of this treacherous predicament.

"Darling!" Horace's voice made me jump. "You cheated! You're dressed! I wanted to dress you while I caressed you!" He dropped the blanket that he was holding in his arms.

Laughing, I suggested that we should return to his place, where I would be happy to let him caress me all night! The night had gotten too cold! *In more than one way*, my logical voice warned. Horace smiled and sheepishly said, "Mind if you turn around? I want to get dressed, too!"

"Horace! I have seen you naked," I said in my most sexy voice. I suddenly did not want to turn my back to him.

"Please?" Horace begged, looking more like an embarrassed teenager after his first time. "I had my back turned when you got dressed!" he argued.

"I love your…," I began to whisper in what I hoped was a sensual voice as I started to turn my back. The stars wavered in the black sky; then a switch was thrown and blackness.

***

I've been drugged! I've been drugged! my addled brain was hysterically shrieking! Slowly, the blackness started to be pulled back, like a soft cuddly blanket slowly being pulled off as you slept. How? I don't do drugs. My words flickered about my subconsciousness like butterflies in a field of wildflowers. Maybe I should rest, perhaps for another minute or so. Rest and maybe I can think more clearly. I started to snuggle into the welcoming darkness, when a voice, a voice that demanded an immediate, loud "Yes, sir! Yes, sir!" roared out, *Sleep and die! Sleep and die! Wake! Up! Now!*

Slowly, I begrudgingly resisted the allure of the darkness and tried to focus on my breathing. When had breathing become so hard to do? After each inhale, I had to work hard to exhale. I needed to stop. I needed a break. I was too weak, too tired. Once again, I found myself being pulled back to my warm, comforting blanket of blackness. Again, I was stopped by that same loud, bone-grating voice. *Stop and die! Breathe, you pathetic lump of flesh! Breathe now!*

Great, I thought, *that miserable, bossy, controlling drill sergeant has returned to take up residence once more in my mind!* I thought it had gone for good after I had left the RCMP training center in Regina. Our drill sergeant was a demon. Even his name was evil. Now, what was his name?

Marty, Monty, Merv, Perv... It flashed into my mind: molester! Yes, that was his name! Moe, no middle name, Lester! No wonder he was the meanest, the most obnoxious drill sergeant to ever put on the uniform. He lashed us daily with words shouted from the most grating voice I had ever heard! Now it was back in my head, barking orders at me. Could this possibly get any worse?

Leave me alone! I thought miserably, even as I started to instinctively obey his orders. Breathe. In and out. In. Out. In. Out. Slowly, my groggy brain's synapses were turning on, one by one. The first thing I noticed was the air; it was heavy with a moldy dampness. Am I buried? This thought was accompanied by a large dose of fear. Fear started to pump adrenaline through my veins. Sluggishly, more of my brain's synapses fired up.

A soft tinkling sound could be heard coming from somewhere nearby. *What is that noise?* Unsuccessfully, I tried to peer through varying shades of red. I could not make out anything. Was I partially buried? *Jesus H. Christ, are you that brain dead? Goddammit, cadet, open your eyes! Now!* yelled my obnoxious Sergeant Moe Lester!

"Shut up!" I moaned. "Not a cadet!" But, like the obedient cadet that I was, I focused my attention on this new task. My eyelids felt so heavy, as if bricks were sitting on them. Struggling, I pulled them open just a crack. I saw tiny particles, like miniature stones. Coarse brownish material provided the foundation for these tiny particles of various sizes. *Hmm, dirt,* I thought dispassionately. *Maybe I am lying in an open grave.* Uninterested, I forced my eyelids to rise up to half mast. This allowed my eyes to see more of this dirt that I was part of. I saw that the dirt stretched out from me, seemingly without end. Not a grave? Ground? I lifted my head a little to take in more of my surroundings. Large cardboard boxes gradually came into focus. Slowly, each box started to spin erratically around me. The ground I was lying on started to roll up and down. Nausea hit my stomach. Bile started to boil up along my esophagus. Hot acid-fueled bile was threatening to spew out of my mouth like lava out of an erupting volcano. I clenched my teeth, in part to keep my stomach contents where they belonged, and in part to keep my teeth from clacking together like castanets. The noise was hurting my head. Heaped inside of these slowly oscillating boxes were odd pieces of clothing, some new and some long outdated. *Where did these clothes come from? Why are they here?* my sleepy, inquisitive voice dreamily inquired.

A faint smell wafted up my nostrils, tantalizing my olfactory epithelium. Puzzled, my brain sluggishly tried to identify the scent. My thought processes were still slow and halting like a child's first steps. I closed my eyes to stop the boxes and ground from spinning and rolling. My body started to float off once more toward the comforting black blanket that I yearned to wrap myself in and feel no pain. Peaceful oblivion.

Do you need your ass kicked, you pathetic excuse for an investigative reporter? Sergeant Moe Lester's loud, grating voice mocked my surrender. Anger, both friend and nemesis, stirred within me at this final insult. Anger was not going to allow this travesty to continue. Anger jolted my body like a stock prod. My body twitched and pushed away that oh so comfortable, desirable soft blanket offering painless bliss.

The persistent wafting scent continued to tickle my consciousness. *Oh my God! Gasoline!* surged through my brain. Fear tasered my body with another surge of adrenaline, fifty times the dose of epinephrine one would receive on an emergency ward! My body jerked and trembled. Gone was my blissful unconsciousness; I was present in the now, frighteningly alert. I realized that I was lying on a dirt floor. My cheek, eye, nose and the side of my mouth were pressed onto the packed earth. Little puffs of dust emitted with each exhalation from my nose.

My jeans felt damp. Did I wet myself? What would Horace think? *Are you fucking crazy? What will Horace think? He's the bastard that did this to you, girl! Fuck him! I hope you pissed on him while you were at it!* Anger was fully unleased and was raging to exact payback. *Payback's a bitch, isn't it! Watch out, Horace, your time is running out! I am coming for you!* I had to hand it to my anger – it did make me feel a little better. I was not just going to take whatever Horace had in store for me lying down! *FYI, you are lying down!* whispered a snarky voice. I realized, with relief, that my jeans were absorbing dampness from the dirt floor.

Feeling cramped and uncomfortable, I tried to sit up. *What the fuck?* My analytical brain was back, alert and operating at max speed but with a sailor's mouth. Incredulously, I discovered that my wrists were tied together behind my back. With a little more effort, I discovered that my hands were also bound to my ankles! "I'm hogtied!" I croaked. Fear gripped me and squeezed my chest. My breathing once more became labored. Panic! I had to get free! "Who did this to me?" I croaked.

Are you really that inept, or is it the chloroform-soaked cloth that Horace held over your face making you sound so stupid? Stupid, stupid, stupid! my investigative voice berated me. Tears silently dribbled out of my eyes. I remembered. I remembered my unease at turning my back to Horace so he could get dressed. His sudden shyness to dress in front of me. Yes, I had to admit that I was failing as an investigative reporter. Maybe Lou and even Tyrell were correct when each had discounted me ever being an investigative reporter. For Lou, the job was too hard, too dangerous for a woman. Tyrell believed it was absurd to even entertain the thought of women as reporters! Maybe it wasn't sexism; maybe investigative reporting is beyond a woman's capability.

Again, anger shot through me like a lightning bolt. I was fully awake and alert. Yes, I was furious for even entertaining the thought that this task was beyond my capabilities. With my outrage came my resolution that I would not, absolutely would not, be beaten by Horace. I was going to beat Horace. I was going to win. Time to get free!

Before I could set to work on getting free, I became aware of strange soft sounds. Tap, tap, tap. I slowly turned my head away from the boxes, seeking the source of this sound. At first, I noticed a very large, wet, flat stone lying near the opposite wall. I saw water droplets hit the stone's hard surface with a minuscule splash. Tiny microscopic water particles flew outward, striking the dampened ground that surrounded the rock. I looked up. I saw a very old-looking pipe that appeared to be flimsily attached to the ceiling. My eyes were drawn to a very slim slit that was slowly birthing another water droplet. As I watched, the water droplet grew larger and larger and larger until gravity was able to pull it from the small crack in the water pipe. Down, down, down came the perfectly formed water droplet.

One mystery solved; but my initial fear, the location of the gasoline, demanded my full attention. I needed to see more. I needed to move. I jerked my trussed-up body over to my right side. Pain like a thousand sharp needles shot through my arms and my legs. Panting, I closed my eyes.

Slowly, the pain eased, became tolerable. I felt my body start to lose its attachment to earth's gravitational pull. My drill sergeant's antagonizing voice barked, *No broken limbs! Quit being such a wuss! Find where that smell is coming from! Now!* My eyes popped open. I was facing the wet stone and something else… wooden stairs!

I slowed my breathing. I saw, in front and a little to my left, some old wooden stairs that rose from the dirt floor, disappearing into darkness. *Into a deserted house*, my observant mind mused, *that is situated in a deserted farmyard where you and Horace had just made love under the stars!* I remembered the tenderness of Horace's lovemaking. I remembered his plans for us. Tears again filled my eyes. Not tears of sadness, but tears of anger at being played for a fool by the man I loved. I was enraged at being suckered into giving myself to this monster. My fury over Geoff's death, my anger over being taken in by Horace, and my rage over my gullibility at accepting everything

Horace said as gospel, rippled through me like multiple taser shocks, each set to maximum!

"How could I?" I moaned despairingly into the dirt floor. The dirt felt cool, like a caress on my right cheek. *You wanted to know the truth. You wanted to know what happened to Geoff. You wanted to be an investigative reporter!* my logical voice taunted me! *You should always be careful what you wish for!* Did I really have time for this internal debate with my other resident voices? Fear was growing within me. Adrenaline, like an arsonist throwing gasoline about a burning building, was surging throughout my body. My muscles were twitching and straining uselessly against the rope that tied my limbs together. *Geoff, please help me*, I mutely cried. Tears were dripping from my eyes, mirroring the water droplets falling from the cracked overhead water pipe. It seemed that even this old house was crying along with me! Lou was right: investigative reporting was too dangerous for a woman. I was such a fool!

A new noise broke into my ruminations. I clumsily twisted my trussed-up body toward the stairs, so I was better able to locate the cause of this new sound. I stoically raised my eyes to stare up at the top of the old wooden stairs partially hidden in darkness. Unexpectedly, a door cracked open, and a feeble light shone down onto the dirt floor. I awkwardly raised my head and gawked, open-mouthed. A large, shapeless thing appeared as if by magic, obliterating most of the faint light that only seconds ago weakly illuminated the stairs. I could see faint rays of light peeking out around this object, highlighting its undistinguishable shape. Were my prayers being answered? Was this God?

Geoff? My guardian angel? "I'm going to be saved!" I whispered to myself. I felt more than heard Moe Lester's voice scoff in annoyance at my stupidity. I kept staring up at this shape that seemed to be suspended in the air. What was that shape? Oh my God, it was a gunny sack! It was the largest burlap sack I had ever seen! Unexpectedly, the sack began to slowly rise up, up into the air and then, like a guided missile, it flew down the stairs! Whoomph! Dust puffed up, accompanying its impact with the dirt floor. A muffled groan emitted from the sack. My irrational brain yelled, *It's alive!* In the next instant, it screamed, *Oh my God it's full of snakes, poisonous snakes! Rattlers!* My insides turned to liquid.

I froze, too terrified to scream.

No, my calm, rational, voice countered. *Snakes don't groan in pain. There is a person inside the bag.* Were Horace and I abducted by the real killer? Had we innocently stumbled into his lair? Had I been wrong about Horace? Again, I felt my drill sergeant's disgusted humph like a slap upside of my head! Okay, I had to admit I wasn't really buying into that theory.

"Ah, darling," Horace's low, sensual voice floated down from the top of the stairs, stairs that he was slowly descending. His husky voice wrapped its cold fingers around my heart as he continued to purr with pleasure. "I see you have returned from dreamland just in time to witness my swansong."

Horace paused his slow descent. He dispassionately regarded the burlap sack that lay close to the foot of the stairs. Horace abruptly hurried down the remaining few stairs, bellowing, "My going away party, my retirement!" He punctuated this announcement with a savage kick to the sack. Another groan emitted from it, weaker this time.

"Stop!" I cried. "What are you doing?"

Horace whirled around and stared down at me, trussed up, lying on the dirt floor. Madness glinted in his gunmetal blue eyes that I had once found warm and caring. Now they were as cold and unfeeling as the color of the metal they represented. "Cathy," he said, shooting an incredulous look at me, "haven't you figured it out yet?" He shrieked, "Tyrell did, and he is a drunken old fool!" Before I could respond, Horace straightened, twisted around and violently jerked the sack down, exposing a battered, bruised and bloodied body. I barely recognized Tyrell's swollen face. His left eye had disappeared into a soft mound of purple flesh. Tyrell didn't move. A white bone jutted out from just below the elbow on his right arm. Horace kicked him hard in the ribs. I heard a snap, like the sound of breaking twigs. Tyrell moaned, softer this time. His broken ribs were making his breathing labored and shallow. His one good eye focused on me.

I am sorry, Missy, his eye seemed to say. *I am so sorry that I got you into this mess! I should have never said anything.*

With tears streaming out of my eyes, pooling into the dirt, I answered that he had nothing to be sorry for.

"Ah, isn't that sweet," Horace sneered as he took in our silent communication. "The old drunk has a crush on you!"

"Please," I cried, "for the love of God!"

"God!" Horace whirled back to face me. "Don't you know, darling, there is no God, there is no happily ever after, there is no heaven, there is just this!" Horace swung his arms

186

around the damp cellar. His anger made his eyes shine with an insane glint. "This," he said, pointing to the assortment of boxes, "this is my duty, my purpose! I have been chosen!"

The voice that had won my young heart a lifetime ago took on the sound of a demonic soul. "I have been chosen to cleanse the world!" His harsh laughter hung in the cellar. Horace raised his arms like a zealot preacher preaching hell and damnation, and screamed, "I am the chosen one!" He stood, silently looking at his surroundings, his words echoing in my head.

Unexpectedly, Horace yanked out a large hunting knife that had been holstered unnoticed in a sheath fastened to his belt. Its large blade glinted menacingly in the dimly lit cellar. Mentally, I shrank back from him, my eyes opened wide with terror. *So, this is how it ends*, my analytical voice calmly observed, *your throat is cut, and you die in this filthy damp cellar*. Horace, in one blurred and swift motion, swung the knife down, slicing through the rope that bound my hands to my ankles.

"Thank you," had spilled from my lips before I could stop myself.

My limbs sprang apart as if they were spring loaded. Instantly, pain shot out from my overextended joints. I lay quivering on the floor, much like Tyrell. My legs would not obey my command to stand. I felt as helpless as a baby.

Horace bent down and roughly grabbed me by my upper arms and pulled me up into a standing position. He held me tightly against his firm body, my head resting against his chest. My legs were trembling so violently that I was not sure if I could remain standing on my own. Horace gently cupped my chin and raised my face so I could look into his eyes. A shiver rippled through me when I saw eyes that were no longer human. Eyes of a killer, a hired killer. When his lips came down on mine and softly kissed me, it was like being kissed by a corpse. There was no warmth. No passion. No love. Horace gently pushed me away from him and released his painful grip on my arms. I stood on quivering legs. "Let me show you the good I have done. Remember, darling, you wanted no secrets between us." His voice mocked the earlier words I had spoken before I knew the extent of the danger I was in. I nodded, too frightened to speak. Horace put his arm around my waist and moved me closer to the stairs, closer to Tyrell, who was lying unmoving on the dirt floor.

Was this my time to escape? To run up the stairs and go for help?

I was fearful that if I attempted this, I would crumble onto the dirt floor in a heap of flesh and bones to lie beside Tyrell. Horace's yelling jerked my attention back to what he wanted me to see and to appreciate. I stared at Horace as he continued to rage.

He reached into an overflowing box and grabbed a coat and held it up for my inspection. "This, this," Horace stuttered. Surprisingly, his voice had increased in volume. Foam, like the whitecaps on a stormy lake, sprayed out of his mouth. I stood rooted to the floor, oblivious to his spit that hit my face. "This belonged to a wife-beater!" He held it up to me for my inspection. "Twenty thousand dollars later and, poof! He was deleted from the human race – accidental drowning." He threw the jacket down in disgust. "These…"

– he reached into another box and snatched up a pair of woman's muddy blue jogging shoes – "would never be worn again by this woman. This woman who wanted for nothing. This woman who was a deceitful whore! She pretended to be going on a run. She left the home her husband had bought for her so she could do what?" Horace glared at me.

Insanity lit his eyes. "What?" he bellowed.

I stood petrified. I had never been so terrified. Horace continued to glare at me, waiting for my response. I murmured, afraid that I would give the wrong answer, "Was she cheating on her husband?"

"Alleluia! Praise the Lord!" he shouted, making me jump. "She will never, never hurt her family again! A park mugging and" – he loudly snapped his fingers that echoed in this underground cellar – "this weak link in humanity's chain was removed forever. I sent her straight to Hell where she belonged with all the other licentious beasts!"

Horace spun around and quickly went to the back of the staircase. He crouched down and pulled out a red plastic jerrycan full of gasoline. *Now we know where the gasoline smell was coming from*, observed my analytical voice. Horace took the can, deftly unscrewed the cap, fitted the yellow nozzle into it, then screwed it tightly back onto the gas can. Satisfied, he stood up, walked over to the boxes, and violently shook the jerrycan as if he was peppering his eggs. Gas sprayed out of the plastic nozzle. The overstuffed boxes were repeatedly doused with gas. Once satisfied, Horace threw the five-gallon plastic fuel can at Tyrell. It bounced off his unmoving body and came to rest on its side. I noticed that some gasoline dribbled out of the spout. Horace didn't notice.

"You know who the real evil people are, Cathy?" Horace asked me as he turned his attention away from his trophies reeking from gas to glare at me. "Cathy, who do you think are the real evil people who need to be eliminated?" Horace's words came slower, more menacing, with a volume so loud that they seemed to bounce around this small room of gas fumes.

Despair was beginning to suck up my hope of surviving this nightmare. My body started to tremble. I was not sure whether it was from fear or from my leg muscles slowly weakening from standing still. Out of the corner of my eye, I noticed a small movement. Shocked, I realized that miraculously Tyrell was attempting to stand!

Horace took my silence to mean impertinence on my part. His fist shot out like a bullet, punching me in the face just below my right eye. I spun around and flew into the gasoline-sprayed boxes, toppling several over with my impact. Instantly, Horace was leaning over me, mere inches from my aching face, and shouting each word slowly, "Who are the real evil people, Cathy?" Foam spilled out from his mouth and sprayed my bruised face.

"Who, Horace? You tell me!" I shouted right back in his face. Anger replaced my paralyzing fear of this man I no longer knew. "I don't know what the fuck you are talking about!" I shoved him back and stood up on legs that were no longer trembling. I glared at him and saw a fiend, not the person I had loved as a teenager. We stood glaring at each other, momentarily at an impasse.

"Reporters!" he yelled so loud that I involuntarily jerked backwards. "Reporters! Reporters are the devil's spawn!" The zealot was back in all its sinister glory. "George Adams" – Horace's voice took on a high-pitched, earsplitting note – "George fucking Adams had the audacity to come here, here, to my home, to my territory – and why? To take me down!"

Cold primal rage instantaneously surged through my body with the realization that Geoff's killer was standing before me. My whole body vibrated with a desire to tear apart this primordial parasite limb by limb. I wanted to beat him into a bloody sludge. I stood taller, straighter, stronger. Horace did not notice. I heard his screaming, but I no longer comprehended his words. I looked at him thinking *Who are you?* My analytical voice came back with brutal honesty. *A fucking bastard is what he is,* I countered. *Hmm, not very lady-like,* my voice of reason cautioned. *I'm thinking more along the lines of a parasitic demon.* Whatever!

White foam in much larger quantities constantly spewed out from his yelling mouth. Wet, slimy globs splattered my arms, my face, my body. I felt repulsed. I shifted my body to my right. I glowered at Horace. Horace glared back at me, oblivious to my sideways movement. I was in a direct line to the stairs with one obstacle: Horace.

I chanced a glance over to where Tyrell was lying. Shocked, I saw that Tyrell, with superhuman strength of determination, had partially struggled to his feet! His courage had taken over his beaten and broken body! His heroism brought wetness to my eyes. My wet eyes signaled that I was ready. I would follow his lead no matter how insane it might seem to me. Horace was not getting away.

Horace, oblivious to Tyrell's movement, continued to rage. I swept my eyes down and then back up to glare at Horace. Suddenly, Horace stopped., The ensuing silence feeling felt like I was being crushed! My body stood erect; like a statue. My emotionless eyes stared through Horace as if he was already dead. Horace registered the change that had come over me. He felt the coldness that emanated from me. Horace stared at me and grinned with realization. I smiled back just as coldly. "Your fiancé…," he started.

"Geoff," I finished with a grin on my lips as I continued to stare through him.

Puzzled, he started to slowly turn around, not wanting to take his eyes off me. Horace expected danger from me and only from me. But he felt threatened from something, or someone, situated behind him. He never even gave Tyrell a nanosecond thought other than to believe there was no threat there. I knew different.

Miraculously, Tyrell was standing erect on unsteady legs that were spread apart to help maintain his stance. Gripped in his left hand was a two- by-four piece of wood that appeared to be about four feet in length. Tyrell looked like he was standing at home plate waiting for the pitch. The pitch: Horace's head. Tyrell waited, aimed and swung the wooden plank like a one-armed batter. The solid piece of wood connected with Horace's skull with a solid egg-cracking sound. Horace's legs buckled and he crumbled to the ground.

Tyrell hit the ground just as quickly. He laid on the dirt floor in a bloodied heap. His body looked like a puppet whose strings had been cut. "Get out," Tyrell said weakly. His bruised and battered good arm had started to slowly move toward his shirt pocket. "Missy, you have to go now. Horace won't be out long. I have to stop him!" his voice was ragged with emotion. Tears flowed from his good eye. "I should have stopped him before, but I was scared!" He looked wretched.

"Tyrell, let me help you," I said, squatting down beside him. "Let me get you out of here. It's over, let the law take over, let the law handle Horace."

"No! Some cops were his clients, too!" Tyrell hissed out; his voice was raspy with pain, making it very difficult to hear his words. His breathing was rapid and shallow. "You must get out of here now!" Tyrell's trembling fingers found his shirt pocket and continued their slow progress inside.

They stopped inside his pocket. Tyrell was drained of all strength. He was unable to pull his fingers back out. I gently held his hand and removed it from his pocket. Clutched in his shaking fingers was a shiny cigarette lighter. Horace moaned and stirred. "Hurry, Missy! He's waking up!" Fear showed on his face. "I am going to stop him once and for all! Please forgive me!" His voice cracked with emotion. "God forgive me!"

I bent down and gently kissed Tyrell's cheek. "There is nothing to forgive! I will never forget the bravest man I have ever known!" I straightened, turned and walked to the staircase. I looked up to the top of the stairs. "Nine steps,"

I whispered. "God bless you, Tyrell," I added, as tears blurred my vision.

I placed one foot on the bottom stair to start my climb. I felt the urgency radiating from Tyrell to get out of the old house, now! I whispered, "Eight to go." I must tell Tyrell's story. I could see bright moonlight shining in through the broken windows. "Seven steps." Then I paused. He's going to set the gasoline on fire! Could I really let him burn himself alive? *Here, I thought you were thinking clearly! Tyrell's going to blow this place to smithereens and if you don't move your ass, you're going to join them!* my analytical voice said sardonically. I increased my speed. "Six, five, four, three, two steps to go." I could see moonlight illuminating a room that I had never seen before. I heard the click of Tyrell's lighter and then a soft, silky woof, the sound of gasoline igniting. "One more step," was my last thought as I was hit from behind with such force that I was airborne, hurtling weightlessly among the flying debris into the dark night, into oblivion.

Now

Tears are running down my cheeks and into my ears. Sobs wrack my body. "Cathy…" I hear a gentle man's voice full of worry. "Are you in pain?" A large hand takes mine and gives it a fatherly squeeze. "You're safe. You're in the hospital." Lou's gruff voice has become even lower and rougher. His eyes glisten with moisture.

"This pain cannot be relieved by any medicine," I sob.

"Do you remember what happened?"

"Yes," I weep, "everything."

"We were waiting for your memory to return."

"Why didn't you just tell me?" I demand. My sobs are turning into hiccups. "Why didn't you just tell me?" My pain accentuates each word I utter.

"Dr Short said it would be better if you remembered yourself. You needed to remember if you would ever have a chance to get over it." Lou replies. Misery is etched across his face. "The police also want a statement from you, but I told them not until you were able to. Dr Short was very firm on this, too." Lou adds, chuckling, "Such a short man, but what a presence! You've had two officers outside of your room each day wanting to interview you and each day they obey Dr Short's orders without argument!"

"I don't want to talk to them right now, Lou. I am so tired."

"Honey, they are not going to be able to talk to you until after Dr Short has seen you and after he gives them the green light. Dr Short also told me to not immediately buzz him when you remembered unless you wanted me to. His advice was for you to wait till he makes his daily rounds."

"Good. Thanks, Lou," I say, squeezing his meaty hand. "I think I just want to sleep." A large, most unlady-like yawn escapes my lips. "Maybe tomorrow." Momentary concern is evident in my next words. "Lou, will you be here?"

"Honey, I was going to be here with the paper's lawyer whether you asked me to or not!"

"Thanks, Lou," I smile. "I am feeling much better knowing that."

"I will get your nurse," Lou begins.

"*I Love Lucy*!" I add, chuckling.

"Yes, Lucy. She'll check your signs and then she'll give you something to help you sleep."

"Hmm, I love hospitals," I mumble sleepily.

Then

Once more, I found myself sitting on the old wooden dock that jutted out over rippling lake water. I turned to look at the person beside me. I was happy to see Mom sitting beside me. "Mom, what are you doing here?" I asked.

"Oh, Cathy," Mom said, squeezing my hand, "it was my time; but, honey, it isn't your time."

"Where are we? I like it here. Why can't I stay? Dad is here, too." My words were stumbling over each other as they rushed to get out.

"I know Dad is here. It is the way it should be, but it's not your time, honey," Mom lovingly told me. "When it is your time, I'll be here with Dad to meet you. Now it's time for you to go back."

"Why are you here?" I inquired.

"It was my time, dear." Seeing my confusion, Mom added, "I want you to do something for me."

"What?" I softly murmured.

"I want you to call me if you need me and I'll come to you. Any time, anywhere! You have earned a guardian angel, and that is me!" Mom said, smiling.

"Great," I moaned, chuckling. "Now I will never be able to hide anything from you." A big smile lit my face. "I love you, Mom," I said, hugging her tightly to me.

"I love you, too!" Mom said with warmth in her voice. "You are the best daughter a mother could ever wish for!" Tears glistened her eyes.

"Oh, Mom, I'm your only daughter!"

Laughing at our long-running family joke, we sat there looking at the water, listening to it lapping at the shore under the dock. With Mom's arms around me, I snuggled into her embrace as if I was a young child, and slept.

Now

"Good morning, Cathy," a cheery voice greets my slowly opening eyes.

"Good morning, Dr Short. What time is it?" I ask, feeling disorientated. Disorientation seems to accurately describe me each morning upon waking.

"I see by your chart and talking to Nurse Lucy and Lou" – I smile, thinking of my brusque editor with a woman in his life – "that your memory returned yesterday! Quite a breakthrough!" cheerfully concludes Dr Short.

"Sometimes no memory is good," I comment sadly. Grief was in my eyes and voice.

"Yes, but memory allows you to heal, and that is what we all want," wisely counsels Dr Short. "Are you ready to talk to the police or do you want to put it off for another day?"

"I will when Lou and the newspaper's lawyer are here," I answer.

These words are already making me feel strong. My life is no longer out of control. I am ready to tell the whole story and to remember the bravest man I had ever met in my life. It was time to speak of Tyrell's heroism!

Dr Short leaves, telling me that he will call Lou. I lie back on my pillows and watch the curtains move slowly in the artificial breeze from the air exchanger. I start going over the events in my mind, so I'm ready to give the police my statement.

"Cathy." Lou's voice wakes me from yet another nap. Am I going to be dozing off forever? Maybe not napping, but power naps, I amend. Yes, I am getting back to my old self. I am once more talking to myself! I wonder if my eagerly advising voices will soon be making their presence felt? One voice, Sergeant Moe Lester, can stay away, thank you very much.

I pull myself up into a sitting position in my hospital bed. Smiling at the memory of my brusque drill sergeant, I look up and see Lou entering my room, followed by a smaller man dressed in a very dark blue suit. Accenting it is a light blue shirt and a paisley tie emphasizing the light and dark blues.

"I want you to meet Mr Nells. Robert is our newspaper's lawyer. I'd like you to follow his advice."

"Sure, Lou," I reply, anxious to put this part of my life behind me.

"There is one more thing, Cathy," Lou cautions, lowering his voice. "Last night, I wrote the story from what you told me. I have given the byline to you and Geoff. I will be sending it to press tonight, after your meeting with the police."

Tears bubble out of my eyes as I remember Geoff talking about this story. "Thanks, Lou, but you wrote it," I argue, "you should have the credit."

"Cathy, you and Geoff were responsible for this story. I just reported what you and Geoff uncovered." Lou's voice is also husky with emotion.

"Thanks, Lou," I say, reaching up to hug him.

"All right, Robert, you can tell our fine police officers that they can come in. Cathy is ready to give her statement with us in attendance."

Robert leaves the room and a moment later returns with two detectives trailing behind him, also dressed in undistinctive suits of similar color. "Hello, Ms Parker," the police officer directly behind Robert says.

"Please, call me Cathy," I add. My hands are already beginning to dampen as I subconsciously tighten my grip on my light hospital blanket that covers me.

"Right." He pauses momentarily, his rehearsed delivery thwarted with my interruption. "You might remember me; I met you earlier in Mr Klassen's office."

"Yes," I interrupt him again. His face reflects surprise. This is going to irritate him, but somehow I can't help myself. Indeed, I have a strange need to prove I am aware of what is currently happening as well as what has happened to me. I want no doubts in anyone's minds that my memory is anything but one hundred percent sound. "You're Detective McNeil. You're with the RCMP."

Smiling, Detective McNeil nods his head, seemingly pleased with me and my display of memory. He points at the other man standing next to him. "And this is my partner. We understand that you are" – he pauses to look at Lou and Robert – "able to remember the events leading up to your hospitalization and that you are able to give us your statement."

"Yes," I say in a voice that has a slight tremor.

"Remember, Josh," Lou warns the officer, "Cathy has legal counsel, and I am also staying here with her." I find myself surprised at Lou being on a first-name basis with this detective. Then, just as quickly, I admonish myself, thinking that while reporting crime and during the investigative reporting of crime, I would expect the Editor of our paper to know several police officers. "This has everything to do with the job Cathy was hired, by me, to do." Lou's voice is hard like steel.

"Don't get your hackles up, Lou," Josh counters, his hands up in the air in surrender. "We have no problem with you being here at this time."

Josh's voice ascertains who is ultimately in charge, making it absolutely clear that it is not Lou!

The increased testosterone in the air from Lou's overt protectiveness of me stirs up my anger. Sighing, I clear my throat and both men turn toward me. I look up at them and sweetly ask, "Detective McNeil, you didn't tell me your partner's name."

"Oh, sorry," Detective McNeil says, somewhat embarrassed. "This is Detective Honest."

"Honestly?" The word is out of my mouth before I can stop myself! I can't help chuckling.

"Yes, Ms Parker," begins McNeil's partner.

"Please, call me Cathy. Honestly, I would prefer you do!" I am unable to quit, laughter bubbling out with my words. The four men also start laughing. The tension of a minute ago is forgotten.

"There is a story behind my name," the detective adds. His voice is serious as the laughter slowly ebbs from the room.

"I am sorry, I don't want you to think I am poking fun at your name." *Honestly*, my analytical voice chuckles. "Please tell me how your name came to be."

"Well," he starts slowly, "when my great-grandparents immigrated to Canada from Czechoslovakia back in the 1800s, they found that there was a very strong dislike, distrust of any person who did not speak" – here he makes quotation marks in the air – "'the King's English'. Quickly, my great-grandfather learned English, and he also changed his last name to sound more English. My great-grandfather shortened Honestichov to Honest."

I interrupt his story, saying, "I am sorry they had to change their name just to be accepted!"

"Yeah, well I find that it is a great ice-breaker when meeting new people!" When he sees Josh's mouth start to open, he warns, "Josh, you don't have to tell Cathy my first name!"

"I think that is only fair. After all, you know my first name," I say, suddenly very curious as to why he doesn't want to share his first name. Can it really beat his last name? Laughter is once more trying to come out from between my lips. Appeasing my desire to laugh, I smile sweetly at the red-faced detective.

Detective Honest continues, looking sternly at his partner, "Only..." – he pauses for emphasis – "because you have been through so much, I'll share it with you." Once more, he pins me with his light brown eyes and sternly adds, "You must promise to never tell another soul!"

I look over at Lou and Robert, who say with big smiles, "We know."

"I promise." I am smiling in anticipation of a name like Sue or Candice.

"My first name is Conleon." He sees the incredulous look on my face.

He continues, "Con is my dad's name and Leon is short for Leona, my mom's name. It seemed that when my mother learned that she could not have any more children, they both wanted me to bear their names!"

Laughing, I said, "Thank you for sharing your secret with me. I will never, ever divulge it!" I pause, momentarily at a loss for words. *Remember your promise to Tyrell*, my orderly voice reminds me. "Well, let's get at it then, shall we? I often doze off and I'd like to get this done before that happens!"

"Right," Josh and Conleon agreed.

"How do we do this? Do you ask me questions, or do I just tell you what happened?" Sincerity is evident in my demeanor.

"Whichever way you want," they answer together.

Taking a deep cleansing breath, I propose, "I will tell you what happened. Please wait until I am finished to question me."

Smiling, Josh nods and asks, "Mind if I record you?"

"It is fine with me," I reply, and then I turn to Robert, "unless my lawyer objects."

Robert smiles; then, while looking at the two detectives, he says, "If I object to any part, then the recording will not be part of the official record. Remember, my client was almost killed because of these events."

Josh says, "We agree to your terms, counselor."

By the time I have finished recounting the events that led up to and the subsequent actions that resulted with me lying here in the hospital with a concussed brain, the filtered sunlight has dimmed. Lunch had arrived, but with Lou's promise of bringing me my favorite McDonald's meal, I quickly send it back and continue to talk. I take the coffee because, after all, even hospital coffee is better than no coffee!

My recounting of the events over the previous months ends with tears welling up in my eyes, remembering Tyrell. "Tyrell saved me." Tears once more flow quietly from my eyes. "A brave man, a hero, a man who..." – my voice breaks again – "who saved me from a killer!"

"The drunk?" Detective Honest asks incredulously. "I knew him and he's—"

"My savior!" I say vehemently.

"Who did he rescue you from?" asks Detective McNeil.

Is this what police do, ask a question after you've already told them? "A killer, a killer for hire," I reply. My soul is feeling cold and heavy. Pain and grief are all that remains. I yearn for the oblivion of the past weeks.

With memory comes healing! Yeah, but do I really want to experience this pain again? Presently, amnesia is looking much more attractive.

"Who?" Detective McNeil inquires again. "What is the identity of this hit man?"

"Horace Moonie," I whisper. I look at Lou, asking, "Didn't I tell you that already?"

"Yes, it was clear, but we needed it stated once more," adds Detective McNeil. "We have to ensure we are understanding everything you are telling us."

"I thought there was something off with Horace," reminisces Detective Honest, "but whenever I tried to talk to anyone about him, the same comment was offered: 'He's a good neighbor, likes to keep to himself.' The drunk—"

"Tyrell," I say with an edge to my voice.

"Er, yes, Tyrell, he was the only one who appeared to want to talk. I should have been more attentive to him. I should not have listened to others who constantly mocked Tyrell. I am sorry to say I started to believe them. I won't ever do that again," Detective Honest vows as much to himself as to the three people who stand around my bed.

***

The next afternoon, Lou enters my room carrying a huge bouquet of multi-colored flowers. Carefully, he places the gigantic vase on my meal tray, threatening to crumble it under the weight of this enormous bouquet!

Brightly colored carnations, tulips and daffodils are barely contained in the large cut-glass vase. Strategically inserted throughout the bouquet are sprigs of white heather. Given prominent position is one orange gladiolus set in its center! "Lou, they are beautiful!"

"Thanks, we, er, all chipped in," Lou stammers, "you know, the staff at the *WDP*."

"They are lovely, Lou. Please pass on my heartfelt thanks!"

"Do you want company for supper?" Lou asks, his voice all business-like. "I was planning on grabbing a burger at McDonald's, but if you want, I can bring both meals back here so we can eat together."

"Why thank you, Lou," I say, smiling, while still admiring the beautiful bouquet. "But when you return, you will have to move this to my nightstand, otherwise I will have no place to eat!"

Lou walks through the parting in my curtains, chuckling. Why is this bouquet so different from the many other usual bouquets? Why one gladiolus? Why the white heather? Knowing Lou, there must be a reason! Smiling to myself, I begin to lie back and tug up my light green hospital blanket, when I notice a small white envelope peeking out from the carnations. Sitting up again, I reach into the massive bouquet to remove the envelope. I pull out the card. I recognize Lou's handwriting.

"Oh my God!" I cry out as I read Lou's note.

"Cathy," Nurse Lucy's voice comes from the other side of my curtain wall, "are you all right?" Quickly parting the drapes, Lucy stops dead in her tracks, exclaiming, "Oh my God!" and starts to laugh with the realization of the repeated cry. "That is a gargantuan bouquet of flowers!"

"Yes, it is, and along with it I just received great news! I have just found out that I have been promoted to investigative reporter at the *Wheatland Daily Press*!" I proudly announce. I am grinning so hard that my face feels like it is going to split into two any second now.

"Let me be the first of your medical team to congratulate you, Cathy!" Lucy says with heartfelt sincerity. She grabs my hand and gives it a firm handshake. "But please be careful! I don't ever want to see a repeat appearance!" Lucy's voice is husky, as if she is coming down with a cold.

Lucy, changing the subject, asks, "I thought I saw Lou. Wasn't he just here?"

"Yes, he left to pick up supper at—"

"McDonald's," Lucy finishes, smiling. "Well, I certainly hope he remembers to bring me a coffee!" Lucy's demeanor returns to a health care professional, adding, "Tomorrow the drapes come down from around your bed! We'll keep the blinds on the windows partly closed. Dr Short believes it is time to begin to reintroduce you to sunlight!"

"This is great news!" I feel like it is Christmas morning, my happiness flooding my soul, diluting my feelings of grief and sadness from my retelling of the events that almost ended my life. *Dr Short is correct*, I think to myself, *my grief is still present, but it is not as sharp and hurtful as before. Remembering is how we heal.*

"Here, dearie, let me put this absolutely beautiful bouquet over on your nightstand." With a quick, efficient motion, Lucy picks up the flowers and moves them to sit on my nightstand, where I can enjoy their wonderful smells and beautiful colors.

"Thank you," I say, while I press a button on my bed remote. Silently and smoothly, the top half of my bed that had me sitting up slowly lowers to a more comfortable reclining position. "I think I'll just rest till Lou arrives with my supper."

Lucy walks out of my draped-in room. I open the envelope to check out the card. Inside the card I see Lou's almost illegible cursive writing. I can hear Lou's gruff voice as I read his message. *I chose the gladiolus because it symbolizes strength of character, honor and conviction. Cathy, that is you. The heather symbolizes protection from danger. All the best, Lou!* I feel empowered by and in awe of a special man, who happens to be my boss! I close my eyes.

I smell the burgers and fries before Lou enters my room. I get out of my bed and stand beside it. I wait. When Lou enters my room, even before he is able to set the bag down, I fling my arms out and catch Lou in a bear hug! Okay, maybe it is more like a newborn bear hug, but I surprise Lou, who almost drops our cups of coffee!

"Cathy! Careful! I don't want to burn you; this coffee is hot!" cautions an embarrassed Lou, struggling to hold onto the bag containing our supper.

"I love you!" I say with emotion choking my words. "You have made me feel so wonderful! I will always treasure your message. Thank you!"

"Cathy, I am not just flattering you! You are like the gladiolus, strong of character, honorable, and you are driven by your conviction of what is right and wrong. I only wish you all the best in your very bright future!"

Lou carefully sets down the McDonald's bag of food and the tray with two extra large cups of coffee on my hospital tray, while I climb back into my bed. "Your story, 'A New Cash Crop', was featured in the top fold of the front page. It was an instant hit as soon as the paper hit the stands this morning! We have never sold so many papers! You should see the fan mail! You are famous! *WDP* is famous, too!" Lou is so happy that I half expect him to start dancing about my bed. "I will start bringing in your fan mail, a little at a time. You can start responding – and if you want, I can get you an assistant to help you!"

"Lou, with everything that has happened, I could never be happier than I am right now. Thank you and yes, I will take you up on an assistant, at least for the next few weeks."

As we start in on our supper, a familiar voice calls out, "Lou, did you remember my coffee?"

"Oh, man," Lou groans.